"A fresh, new voice . . . Jim [...]
curtain of time to give rea[...]
exciting era of American his[...]
—ROBERT VAUG[...]
the *American Chronicles*

In the 1790s, the Ohio Valley sat on the frontier of a new nation. Life was hard in the untamed wilderness, and civilization was fragile at best. Danger came in many forms—animals, disease, starvation. But the worst danger came from the nearby presence of hostile Indian tribes, who would attack the settlements, massacring all they could find. Because of the frequency and brutality of the raids, trading with the Indians was viewed as treason, carrying a sentence of death by hanging . . .

THUNDER IN THE VALLEY

January 17, 1792. Matthan Hannar had kept hidden for ten days, winding his way upriver, avoiding both the settlers who wanted him at the end of a rope, and the Indians who would scalp any white man on sight. But when he saw Zelda Shaw struggling for her life with a knife-wielding savage, there was no way he could stay in hiding and watch her be killed.

But saving the girl's life brought more problems, because now he had a partner. Now two people had to be protected from the cold, starvation, and those who would kill them both. And Matthan was taking Zelda home, downriver, where the hangman's noose was waiting . . .

"Meticulous attention to detail, time, place, and good old-fashioned storytelling . . . Woolard is an impressive writer who has spun the kind of yarn that is easy to recommend."
—CAMERON JUDD, author of
The Overmountain Men and *Timber Creek*

THUNDER IN THE VALLEY

JIM R. WOOLARD

JOVE BOOKS, NEW YORK

THUNDER IN THE VALLEY

A Jove Book / published by arrangement with
the author

PRINTING HISTORY
Jove edition / August 1995

ISBN: 0-515-11630-0

A JOVE BOOK®
Jove Books are published by The Berkley Publishing Group,
200 Madison Avenue, New York, New York 10016.
JOVE and the "J" design are trademarks
belonging to Jove Publications, Inc.

PRINTED IN THE UNITED STATES OF AMERICA

10 9 8 7 6 5 4 3 2 1

To
Nancy Carroll . . .
for everything.

Prologue

Marietta, Ohio
January 5, 1836

To my son,
Matthan Hannar, Jr.,

The task I face is an onerous one, and I suspect I lack the courage, if not the strength, for finishing it.

No man fancies recollecting those occasions on which he found himself scared nigh onto death, been worried so great his innards hurt, or worse yet, proved himself god-awful foolish. But my beclouded past threatens us anew and may yet imperil what for you is a most promising future. Lord knows such a prospect gnaws at my vitals morning and night.

I have long hankered to jaw with you about the rumors and half-truths making the rounds twixt the locals since you stepped under the political tent by declaring yourself for the Congress.

And therein nests my problem.

You surely are aware of how I can't exchange personals. It's not that I be cold-boned. Somehow feelin's and sentiments always stay my tongue. And since my big black spell back at the harvest moon, a red-eyed drunkard fares better with words than yours truly. In short, I can't abide looking the fool.

Matthan . . . I can't honestly and won't falsely profess amends for what I been guilty of in the past. A man traverses many paths in the precious few years his Maker grants him. Sometimes, with forethought, much sweat, and a heaping dose of pluck, a good man can skirt clear of trouble. Other times, no matter how good a man be, happenings catch him up in a brew of bad tidings that sap most all his strength just to keep plugging along and holding his nose above water.

Your detractors claim I was—and still am and always will be—a liar, a thief, and a traitor because of what transpired back there in the winter of 17 and 92. If any credence is given the backbiting of them who never bark in the light of day, it appears I ungratefully ducked my chance before the bar of justice. Seems I taken out for New Orleans and made my pile of gold in the river trade whilst those few knowing the true story of my supposed foul deeds shed their lifeblood in the Injun troubles of 17 and 94.

I ain't disgruntled over the ease with which many of our townsfolk embrace that side of certain past events. Each and every soul paints pictures of things past with his own brush. And just as surely, most folks find themselves too contrary for ever allowing they might have daubed wrong colors on a few canvasses.

What I must do is set down my own recounting as well as I am able. I wish you no misfortune. You are a good son. You seldom failed to please. You got your chores and your recitations. Even your reading for the law didn't displeasure me once I reckoned it was your prime ambition.

There is also your whelp—my grandson—preying

on me. He is such a savior on mean days. It would certain be the death of me if little Matthan, the Third, ever believed poorly of his "Gan-Paw."

I trust I can sustain a firm hand. My limbs suffer me with the onset of winter, and I struggle with my wind. I study the cold and snow outside the office here at the boatyard and remember long and hard, for the cold was as bitter and the snow even deeper back along the Muskingum in 17 and 92. I can only pray that the elements, instead of hampering my writing, sharpen my memory and my quill.

When I finish, you may do with these papers as you wish. I will take pains and not ramble and wander and burden you with too many particulars. Nonetheless, I must tell enough that you might could well decide that any creature worth its salt, when menaced by danger at every turn, and forced to stand alone, can only follow the trail that unfolds before him, no matter what the Lord serves him up.

'Tis all I have ever demanded of you.

Your loving father,

Matthan Hannar

Matthan Hannar's Recounting

Chapter 1

Morning—January 7, 1792

It has been some forty odd years since the Ballard brothers ambushed me on the seventh day of January, 17 and 92.

Even if I live another forty years, I'll never forgive myself for letting them take such liberties with me. Before the day ended, my whole life turned upside down, never to be the same again.

I can remember everything about that cold clear morning. Before I met up with the Ballards, I was a mighty happy lad marching home along Wolf Creek, downright pleased with anything and everything. And why not? I was warmly garbed in moccasins, linsey-woolsey breeches, buckskin hunting frock, and pelt cap—nothing for courting the fair damsel in, I admit, but no better garments could be had for the hunting trail in crisp weather.

I toted a fine flintlock rifle that morning, a rifle that seldom failed me, and on my back I bore the quarters of the buck deer I'd slain with it just an hour before. And if warm bones, a fine rifle that smelt of burnt powder, and a heavy pack burdened with the meat of a fresh kill didn't come close to heaven on earth, downstream at our home place my stepfather, John Hannar, back from a venture up the Muskingum, and Uncle Jeremiah eagerly awaited my return. I chuckled. No jerked beef or salt pork would grace the Hannar table this night. We'd eat prime buck, and nothing less would do.

It had been a grand morning, and it tickled me I owed the brindle cow for my success. Yesterday afternoon she'd drifted away from her shed. A quick quartering of the ground at the edge of our clearing confirmed she'd moseyed along the north bank of Wolf Creek. I'd suspected right off she could be found grazing in the meadow across the ford a few miles upstream. Even in winter, whenever left unpenned or untended, she sought the last of the good grasses there.

Despite my confidence I followed her path those few miles with sweeping eye and ready gun. Just a few weeks back General St. Clair's army had suffered a horrendous defeat at the hands of the Ohio Indians, and the victors were free to kill and plunder throughout the territory. The cow needed bringing in, but not at the cost of my hair.

She was there in the far reaches of the upstream meadow all right, head down, feeding without a care for anything else. I stood firm in a copse of oak and eyed the woods about her. Satisfied she was alone, I loped across and slapped a lead rope round her neck. Just then I sighted the deer tracks. Four sets of hoofprints bordered the trees in each direction in an irregular, yet steady line. Each print seemed of the same size and depth. My heart quickened. They'd all been made by one animal.

Squatting, my probing finger found the freshest of the hoofprints firm-edged with only tiny leaf bits and little upturned dirt in the center. That made them no more than a half dozen hours old. The others, if aged by their content and how much frost and sun had blurred and flattened the edges of them, looked one, two, and possibly three days old. Their message sounded clear as the peal of thunder on a quiet summer afternoon. Coming first round the eastern hill in front of me, the solitary deer browsed northward every morning.

It was a perfect setting for the whitetail. The trees shielded the rising sun well past dawn, creating shadows through which he fed his way with a feeling of security for a morning drink at the creek. The animal, unless disturbed or spooked, would no doubt continue his sunrise ritual tomorrow. And I would be here awaiting. I led that poor brindle cow home at a pace just short of a gallop, shooting appetite thoroughly whetted.

Even the poorness of the evening didn't dampen my spirits. Uncle Jeremiah, tortured by a lame ankle, acted cross and snappish as a she-bear guarding her cubs, and Stepfather, just that day back from his Muskingum venture, proved no better company. The cough he'd acquired in the Harmar Indian Campaign of 17 and 91 doubled him up on the rope bed opposite the hearth. I tended the stock and quietly sought the husk bed in the sleeping loft.

Uncle Jeremiah, bless him, recovered in time and wished me Godspeed next morning. Out and under way before first light, I waded the creek below where the shoulder of that eastern hill nudged the opposite bank and padded for a spot between two large elms from which the length of the meadow could be seen. Stones gathered from along the edge of the water and mounded between the trees provided a solid shooting rest for my flintlock. I settled in, wedging a shoulder against one of the elms, and removed the deerskin cover from the lock of the rifle. With the hammer pulled to half cock, the frizzen opened freely. I primed the firing pan with fine grain powder, closed the frizzen, and snugged the hammer all the way back.

A white oak down at the other end of the meadow stood out clearly in the graying dawn, a perfect sighting target. By candlelight at the cabin I'd loaded the rifle with a full seventy-two grain charge of powder. Though I'd hold fire till my prey reached the midpoint of the meadow for a sure shot, that first shot had to be hard and telling. There'd be no time for a second before the deer gained the trees close at hand.

I started my watch. Spotting deer required considerable skill and Uncle Jeremiah had schooled me well. First you looked at the whole meadow at the same time, not just some likely section of it. That way, any movement stood out and told you where to look in earnest. Otherwise you trusted your ears, which, in light of how quietly deer sometimes skulked about, greatly limited the likelihood of making a successful kill.

I caught the flicking of a pair of large ears above a screening of brush long before the white-tailed buck pranced into the meadow and commenced feeding. He nibbled at twigs and small branches along the forest fringe, pausing every once in a while to scan his surroundings. A wary devil and for good reason. An antler stub flopped loosely on the side of his head and a long scar zigzagged down his neck. Some scuffle had taken a pretty severe toll on him. He fed his way patiently toward me, and I just as patiently let him come on.

He got within fifty yards when all of a sudden his tail twitched, his head popped up, and he stared straight in my direction. I held my breath. I hadn't moved. No wind stirred. He hadn't scented me. Then his ears jiggled and I knew some far-off noise too faint for my hearing was bothering him.

He listened long and hard. Eventually, deciding nothing really threatened him, he turned his head and stretched for a high branch, fully exposing the base of his throat and the top of his shoulder. I drew a bead on that juncture of his body and squeezed off my shot.

The slam of the ball buckled his knees. His tail dropped and he lunged for the trees in a staggering death run.

I let him go. Sticking with Uncle Jeremiah's

teachings, I made ready in case the gunshot's echoing roll attracted hostile Injun attention. I scampered upright behind the elms, greased linen patch and metal pick from the box in the stock of the flintlock gripped between my teeth.

I measured with powder horn and charge cup, and with gun resting butt first on the ground, poured the precise charge of French black down the barrel. Next down the barrel, swathed in the greased linen patch and powered by a thrust of the hickory ramrod, went a ball from my shot pouch. I tamped patch and ball home and reseated the ramrod inside the thimbles and groove under the barrel with a slight *snick* of noise.

A flick of the wrist swept the butt of the rifle off the ground and balanced the weapon in my left hand with the lock at belly level. An off-hand tug set the hammer at half cock and exposed the firing pan. The tail of my hunting frock served as a handy rag for wiping clean the pan, the flint held by the jaws of the hammer, and the frizzen. A jab and twist of the metal pick reamed clean the touchhole in the bottom of the pan. Priming the pan with more powder completed the reloading, and off I went after the whitetail.

I disdained the open meadow, circled the shoulder of that eastern hill, and trotted northward along the bottom of a dry ravine. At the point I figured the buck entered the trees on the far hillside I started climbing. My luck held true. I topped the hill and over left of me, short of the crest, lay the buck, glazed eyes wide open, blood pooled 'neath his scarred neck.

I gutted and skinned him hastily, dressed the quarters and bundled them in the hide. Something had alerted that wild dead creature—some unnatural sound—and that festered in my craw. Being a fair distance from home and probably the only white man out and about for miles, I felt lonely and exposed even with close-by trees and brush masking my presence. The safety of the cabin and the companionship of Stepfather and Jeremiah seemed all at once of paramount importance.

I abandoned the rest of the carcass and backtracked for Wolf Creek. Early on I stuck behind good cover, checked my back trail, and moved at a slow, careful pace. But as a boy is prone when the winter sun warms his homeward-bound backside, my stride lengthened and the worry faded the farther I walked and the more I dreamily relived the morning hunt. How I fairly wanted to burst out and whistle a tune. I marched past the creek bend short of our cabin as carelessly as a love-befuddled stag in the rut.

And there stood the Ballard brothers, Timothy and Joseph, one on either side of the footpath, rifles leveled and centered on my breastbone.

"Freeze right thar," Timothy ordered.

I done as I was told. Let me tell you, those Ballards never were anything much to look at, what with their sparse black beards, long noses, beady gray eyes, and flesh white as milk. On top of that their hats drooped with age, animal blood stained their greatcoats, and their leather boots were badly worn at sole and heel. They smelt of wood smoke and manure and appeared duller than opossums in a motherly way. Some joked on them. But not I. Uncle Jeremiah'd admonished me once these two boys enjoyed a lick of dirty work long as the pay followed right after in gold coin. Little, if anything, was beneath them.

"Matthan," Timothy said, "us'ens won't harm you lest you get contrary. Now Joseph is goin' round behin' you an' lay holt on that thar rifle. . . . You understan'?"

I nodded my head.

"You put that rifle butt agin the groun' an' keep lookin' me right in the face. You look anywheres elst an' I'll blow a hole in your brisket. . . . You understan'?"

I nodded again.

"What about his knife an' tomahawk?" queried Joseph.

"Pitch 'em," Timothy responded.

I stood quietly while they disarmed me.

Timothy shifted his feet. He fixed me with a gaze cold as dead ashes and said slowly, "Now, Matthan, we all gonna head down fur the edge of your clearin'. I'll be in front an' Joseph straight behin'. . . . You understan'?"

He drew still another nod from me.

"Now, Matthan, donna get your pride up over this an' try somethin' stupid. Donna fret 'cause we tracked an' taken you so easy. And donna try warnin' your step-paw. If'n you give out with a peep or taken a misstep, Joseph's gonna blow your backbone in two. . . . You understan'?"

I studied on his words—no fool this one. Nevertheless, I allowed as how once we were in single file and moving, the deer meat shielding my back might stop a shot from Joseph's gun and give me the opportunity to pounce on Timothy. But Timothy, studying on how I was right big for a lad of ten and nine years, thought right with me. He smiled a yellow-toothed smile.

"Best drop the pack before we leave out of here, Matthan. We wouldn' want anythin' twixt your backside an' a bullit, would we now?"

Respect for Timothy growing by the instant, I slid the straps from my shoulders and let the bundle of deer meat tumble into the dirt at my heels. The two of them had me in a box without a lid. I could only silently curse myself for letting them put me there without a struggle.

"Leave us go. Big people be awaitin'," snapped Timothy.

Chapter 2

We started down the footpath as my captors ordered, Timothy in the lead, then me, then Joseph. Being marched home at rifle point, vitals a-jumble, mouth dry as an empty bucket, hands clammy, legs wobbly, made for an unsavory experience. The awareness my captivity stemmed solely from my own carelessness and foolishness didn't make it any easier either.

What upset me most were my fears for Uncle Jeremiah and Stepfather. I sensed that since I'd not personally slighted the Ballards or their as yet unknown "big people," they wanted me—needed me—under their control for getting at those I loved the most.

I kept my wits about me by speculating as to who or what had caused my predicament. Who were the Ballards' "big people"? What did they have against us Hannars? What did they have in store for us?

Much I didn't know. But I knew the Ballards, and with that bit of knowledge and some fast brain work I soon answered some of the questions puzzling me. My captors disliked hard labor and mostly hired out as long hunters, scouts, and guides, occasionally tracking down lawbreakers for the High Sheriff of Washington County. Like all men of the trail, they wore moccasins when traveling any great distance, so they wouldn't lay tracks instantly telling the redskins white men were afoot roundabouts. Yet both Timothy and Joseph wore flat-soled leather boots this morning which likely indicated they'd come from not far off, probably Waterford or Fort Frye, the closest settlements. So it seemed a good bet someone from one of those places with gold coin handy had hired the Ballards and sent them to fetch young Matthan Hannar. But why? We Hannars, by nature closemouthed upcreekers who farmed and trapped, shunned contact with them who preferred their living shoulder-to-shoulder. What contact we had with townsfolk resulted from necessity. I frantically fished my memory for some offense on our part that could have set the local populace against us.

What I remembered right then and there formed a raw lump in my gut. I commenced praying silently, praying my captivity didn't concern Abel Stillwagon and Stepfather's trading ventures with the Ohio Indians up north. If the settlers currently forted up over on the Muskingum at Fort Frye knew of their ventures, particularly the most recent, occurring as it had after St. Clair's bloody defeat at the hands of those same Ohio Indians, we Hannars indeed faced days of desperate bad trouble . . . perhaps even a public lynching.

The lump in my gut hardened and grew when Timothy's "big people," none other than Colonel Van Hove and his son, Lansford, stepped from the trees crowding the path. The Van Hoves headed by stature and wealth the townspeople of Waterford and the newly built Fort Frye. The colonel forsook the comfort of his private abode with great reluctance. Hirelings tended his land holdings and operated his Wolf Creek grist mill. Even here in the raw wilderness the elder Van Hove dressed in silver-buckled shoes, silk stockings, and short breeches, leather belt with huge silver buckle, white linen shirt, and broadcloth coat. He'd armed himself with a .66-caliber, short-barreled, silver-decorated rifle best suited for close-range shooting. Lansford, though more attired for the outdoors in fringed buckskins and beaded moccasins, sported a belt with a huge brass cinch, and the stock of his long rifle was studded with shiny brass inlays. Such dandified clothing and flashy weapons, all showing little use and wear, told a lot about the Van Hoves. They were townspeople who sallied over the far hill away from the protection of their fellow men only when aroused and bent on punishing the transgressions of those of lesser attainments.

My heart sank. For the Van Hoves to stoop to hiring the Ballards, whom they despised, and trek this far from the succor of Fort Frye, they indeed believed us Hannars guilty of a gross sin. It couldn't be anything but the trading with the Injuns.

We halted before the elder and younger Van Hove,

the muzzle of Joseph's rifle bumping my spine. I watched them closely. Of the two I believed Lansford, more so than his father, downright evil-tempered and mean. The colonel's son had been present when we'd purchased our tract of land from the Ohio Company at Marietta. His demeanor that day, and his mouthings at a chance meeting later upriver, had prompted Jeremiah to remark back then, "That boy be a bother without tryin' real hard. The colonel smothers him an' won't give him anythin' important for to do. He yaps 'bout goin' off and fightin' the Injuns, but he's too big a coward for that. Yet he's terrible impatient an' he's determined somehow he'll maken the hero an' prove the colonel misjudges him. Watch out for him. He's cold as river ice inside. He don't care for no man. Given the chance, he'll kill you for personal gain, sure as day. . . ." Jeremiah's words from the past fattened my worries.

"He give you any trouble?" Lansford asked Timothy.

"Naw, easy as pickin' a hickory nut offen the ground," chortled Timothy.

"Good. Let's—"

"Quiet, Lans," the colonel interrupted. "I'm in charge here. You all have your orders and I want them obeyed without question!"

The colonel squinted at me past the fat rimming his cheekbones. "If you wish to live, you follow orders too. I could have you shot now and not a soul would hold me at fault."

The colonel squared his shoulders.

"Time be a-wasting. Let us gather the other two scoundrels. I want all three of them over at the fort before evening."

I garnered a little solace from that. At least the colonel would imprison us at Fort Frye and not kill us of his own accord. We would be brought before a court of the people. But I hadn't been born under a rock. A public trial didn't bode well for us either. Refuting whatever proof the colonel had against us would be a hard proposition. He seemed almighty sure of himself just now, almighty sure.

"Let us perform our appointed task, my brothers," the colonel trumpeted, turning for the clearing and our cabin.

He led the way, followed by Lansford and Timothy, then me with the younger Ballard's rifle at my backside. Showing no fear of anyone inside the cabin, the colonel marched across our clearing till he was a few yards beyond the front entrance, stopped, and with a motion of his hand positioned Lansford and Timothy directly before the door, leaving Joseph and me an equal distance from those two as himself.

"Hello, the cabin," bellowed the colonel.

Silence.

"Hello, the cabin," the colonel repeated.

Silence.

"I be a man of great patience, but it is wearing thin," proclaimed the colonel. "If I don't have an answer by a count of three, Matthan, who we hold, will be shot dead. One . . . two . . ."

My breath caught in my throat.

"What you want with us?" Stepfather demanded from inside the cabin, ending the colonel's count before my heart burst.

"I want you and that old goat in there with you out here on that stone stoop, unarmed, double-quick! Any sign of delay or resistance and you can dig a grave for Matthan. . . . Move!"

"I'm comin'," Stepfather announced loudly. "Don't shoot Matthan. Don't get carried away on me now. I'm comin' alone. Jeremiah's leg is hurt an' he can't walk. But he won't cross you an' cause you to hurt the boy. Here I come."

The plank door swung open and Stepfather stepped onto the stoop, hands held away from his flanks. One glance and I knew why he'd been caught off guard so easily. Splotches of blood mottled his shirt. That horrible racking cough had been ravaging him again. Never had his features been so gray and drained. He was hacking his life away and he looked it.

He swallowed twice, forestalling another bloody outburst, and stuck out his chin as Lansford lifted his rifle from waist to shoulder and drew a bead on him. A solid man rendered thin by illness and suffering greatly, Stepfather stood barefoot on the stone doorstep, devoid of fear. I was never prouder and never loved him more. He gave no quarter and would beg none from the likes of the Van Hoves and the Ballards.

"Easy, Lans," cautioned the colonel.

"What can be done for you, Colonel?" asked Step-father.

The colonel threw back his head and laughed, and with his red beard, considerable girth, and spindly legs, he reminded me of a crowing rooster. "John Hannar, the proper question be what can be done for you and your'en. What I can do is haul the lot of you over yonder and call a public meeting tonight at the fort . . . and denounce the three of you for treason . . . treason for selling gunpowder and whiskey to the very red devils who butchered the troops of my noble friend, General St. Clair. I intend to hang you all or have you all shot. What do you say about that, John Hannar?"

"What proof you got I acted treasonable, Colonel?"

"I have in my possession the sworn statement of the honorable Tice Wentsell," the colonel retorted haughtily.

My innards fairly turned over.

We were doomed. Wentsell, a feared and respected border fighter, spied on the redskins and their doings for General Putnam of the Ohio Company. No one challenged or questioned the word of Wentsell.

"Mr. Wentsell," the colonel related, "oversaw you leading a string of packhorses for the headwaters of Pataskala Creek and followed you unseen. He saw you meet with Abel Stillwagon. When you left for home, he observed Stillwagon and a stiff-legged rowdy advancing the powder and corn liquor deeper into Shawnee country. What do you say about that, John Hannar?"

"I say your eyes be brown 'cause you're full of horse manure, Colonel," Stepfather countered.

Colonel Van Hove was clearly insulted.

"Why you worthless, backwoods traitor. Why shouldn't I hang you this instant? . . . Well, why shouldn't I?" the colonel raged angrily, spittle dotting his lips and the hairs of his red beard.

Those next few moments were so utterly quiet I swear I could hear the wisp of smoke from the cabin's hearth rubbing the top stones of the chimney as it floated free into the sky. My chin trembled. If Stepfather pushed the colonel far enough, we might all die right here in our own dooryard.

The colonel got his answer all right, but not from Stepfather as he expected. The shutter of the window on his side of the cabin slammed open and the barrel of a musket slid across the sill and centered on his ample belly. "There won't be any killin' today, fat man, lessen you're for meetin' the Maker first," rasped Uncle Jeremiah.

The colonel bristled at this new insult. At the same time a frown shown on his face. Jeremiah's jumping in had disrupted his carefully planned punishment of the dire sins of us Hannars, and he wasn't sure how to proceed. But no matter how much he might be chastising himself for being neglectful about Uncle Jeremiah, and no matter how powerfully anxious he might be for delivering us our just dues, he didn't favor rashness that would give Jeremiah reason to shoot him in the belly.

I glanced at Lansford. A wolfish sneer bared the

younger Van Hove's teeth. The bastard! He would
see us killed no matter what.

"Take the old man, Colonel," Lansford commanded.

The uncertain colonel tilted his gun—I've always
believed he meant to turn and confront his son
before he lost control of the whole affair. But Uncle
Jeremiah saw it differently.

And that's what counted for all concerned.

Jeremiah blasted away with the musket and
winged the colonel. The ball smashed the colonel's
shoulder and flung him in a half circle, discharging
his gun. His errant bullet lanced the hip of our boar
hog in the pen by the horse shed and that stud pig
let out a squeal of agony heard for miles.

Lansford had his chance for maken the hero.

He shot Stepfather square in the face . . . and
my whole life flew to pieces.

"Git, Matthan!" Jeremiah yelled as he ducked out
of sight below the sill of the window.

Timothy Ballard sprinted for the cabin door to get
at Uncle Jeremiah before he could reload. Lansford
followed him, knife in hand.

Jeremiah's peril goaded me into action. I spun
around, clasped the barrel of Joseph Ballard's rifle
with my left hand, and yanked the muzzle past my
waist, jerking him forward onto his toes. In his
surprise (he had been watching the events in front of
the cabin without concern for his prisoner), Joseph
triggered off his piece. A haze of powder smoke
billowed between us. I thrust the point of my right

elbow hard against his jaw and shattered bone. He freed the rifle, grabbed at the source of his pain, and collapsed at my feet.

Still clutching the smoking barrel of his rifle, I heard the booming report of a gun inside the cabin. I screamed Jeremiah's name.

No answer.

I screamed his name again.

Then Lansford appeared in the opening of the window and I couldn't help myself. I turned and taken to heel.

"We'll get you, Hannar! We'll get you!"

Overcome by plain, honest-to-God fear, I pounded up the footpath past the discarded bundle of deer meat, pounded round the bend in the creek, and pounded across the stream, feet driving water spouts higher than my waist, destination unknown and totally unimportant. I slipped and fell at the edge of the water. My pelt cap flew off and a knee banged on a rock. No pursuit could be seen or heard. That didn't deter me. Fear was a powerful spur. I lunged up the bank, ignoring the brush that ripped my sleeve and severed the strap holding my powder horn, and darted into the trees. And ran . . . and ran . . . and ran some more. Barren branches lashed my face and hands with red welts; spasms knotted my leg muscles; a hot band of pain encased my chest: I paid them no heed. I fled with the recklessness of a stampeding buffalo.

I managed another mile before topping a swell of ground fronting a pocket of trees. Here I stumbled.

Down the far side of the swell I went on my rump, gun clattering after my careening body. I slid to a halt and rested on my back, too tired to run anymore.

The fear drained out of me. I thought of Stepfather and Jeremiah and grief brought on the tears. They streamed unchecked down my welted cheeks. I forgot about running away and wept till my eyes ran dry of their own accord.

After that I went crazy for a while, crazy as a fox with the wild fever, the fever so maddening he bites at everything—trees, rocks, even his own limbs. I flailed the stony ground with my hands and cursed and damned Stepfather for bringing the law down on us. I cursed and damned God Almighty for letting Stepfather and Jeremiah die at the hands of the Van Hoves and the Ballards. And I cursed and damned my own stupidity and foolishness for being the real cause of it all.

The swelling pain in my hands made me cease the thrashing and swearing. I cradled Joseph Ballard's rifle in my arms and rocked back and forth as if I held a baby, moaning and blubbering in my own private hell, as lost as a man adrift on a stormy sea.

Chapter 3

I rocked for hours. Gray clouds covered over the sky and a gusting wind blew up a rain that matted hair and started teeth chattering. Too spent and empty for caring if anyone hunted me, I ignored the rivulets collecting in the open pan of Joseph Ballard's rifle. I'd no powder for it anyway. I sat wide-eyed, seeing nothing.

Though wet and shivering, I stayed put. If I moved I might flee again in sheer panic and waste whatever measure of strength and presence of mind still in my possession. Yet I knew I couldn't stay there in the darkening forest forever. Sooner or later they'd be after me, and not a soul remained who'd give me a helping hand. And my chances, with an empty rifle and no gunpowder, no food, not even a covering for my head, weren't worth bragging about.

All of Jeremiah's training called for careful planning and decisive action if my life was to be spared. But bitterness and grief and fear muddled my brain. My quandary was such I couldn't sort out what needed doing first.

If only Jeremiah were there with me. He'd always been my rock. His advice had never failed me. I asked myself what that wise old sage would do. Would he surrender at Fort Frye and plead his innocence? Or would he cut south for the Ohio River? Or would he sneak up the Muskingum into Indian country? And what about the supplies I needed? How would Uncle secure powder, food, and dry clothing?

But try as I might, I'd no ready answers. A shelled cob of corn had more kernels of wisdom. I could only repeat the same question—what would Jeremiah do?—endlessly, over and over, again and again . . . over and over, again and again . . .

A noise from somewhere.

Or was there?

I looked up and gasped aloud.

Gray beard and hair haloing his weathered countenance, Uncle Jeremiah sat cross-legged on the swell of ground I'd tumbled down earlier, calmly puffing on his pipe carved in the shape of a sea nymph.

A shake of the head in disbelief produced no change. He remained right dead center in front of me. He wasn't really there. I knew that. He was a figment of the mind—something existing only in my eyes, a quirk spawned by utter desperation and loneliness.

But I really didn't concern myself with all that. If I'd gone loony, so be it. How I craved his understanding and guidance.

Uncle took the pipe from his mouth. "Nephew, there be plannin' an' doin' required of you. First, though, rest easy. The Lord ain't abandoned you. It just appears He has. He'll always be with you in spirit and teachin's, just as I will. Don't forget that! You stick with our teachin's an' you got a solid chance of gettin' clear of this here silly fuss."

Jeremiah sighed heavily. "I loved my brother John. But he owed for his deeds one way or the other an' he knowed it. Dead be dead no matter where, an' John and me was gettin' on anyways, him from the gallopin' cough an' me from age. That's why I winged that strutter of a colonel, even though I was sure it would likely get both of us kilt. I reckoned on you having the sense God give geese, that you'd make your break, an' you done it. That's what counted, your gittin' away.

"I also reckoned the Ballards an' Lansford would be obliged to cart the colonel to Fort Frye first an' return for you later. Howsomever, Lansford will head a meetin' tonight, never doubt. He'll tell all who will lend an ear how loathsome we Hannars be an' how I shot the colonel, an' tomorray a troop of our uproused militia will be frothin' to hound the life out of you. The God-fearing will follow him out of blind anger an' hate for anyone that dared for an eyewink connive with the red Injuns. But even the dunderheads what maypass stands around durin' mean times wringin' their hands an' stammerin', 'oh gosh, oh gosh,' not knowin' what to do next, will side with Lansford this time round. The crowd will tender

them the courage they can never find themselves."
Uncle paused and drew on his pipe. I said nothing,
totally entranced by his words.

"Matthan, you can't saunter over to that there fort
an' plead your innocence, innocent though you be. I
couldn't let them jail you there. Them folks be scart
as hound pups in deep water that ain't learnt to
swim, an' scart folks don't show good sense. I've
taught you that, ain't I? Yep, they'd shoot you or
hang you. Nosiree, there be no help nor feelin's for
you in the den of the Van Hoves. Well, what elst be
there for you?"

He continued quickly. "You can't strike for the
Ohio by your lonesome from here neither. Too many
Injun haters thataway who'll be huntin' you once
Lansford spreads the word, an' trust him, he'll
spread it fast and thick.

"You knows," he said, dipping his shaggy head at
me. "You ponder on it, ponder on it hard. The one
man in all of Ohio that might be somewhat joyed at
seein' you is that treacherous, big-nosed Abel Stillwagon. Quite a turnabout that is, ain't it? He's really
the cause of most of your trouble. But, all in all, he'd
likely welcome you since you could tell him what's
happened down thisaway. An' since you was listenin'
in on me an' your step-paw from the loft back aways,
you know where to rendezvous with him. Ponder on
it some! He'll want to be taken them furs he'll have
outta the country another way instead of down the
Muskingum as planned, won't he now?"

Jeremiah peered down at me and sucked rapidly

on the sea nymph pipe. "You gotta do it my way, Nephew. A backwoodser havin' a fair piece to traipse with dangers all about can't be touchy 'bout who he asks for help. Abel ain't trustworthy, but he be a first-rate fightin' man, an' you could lower the strain offen him an' that clubfooted little ruffian that sides him. You can taken John's place an' help 'em haul them furs where they can be sold off. An' once you're out on the wide Ohio, you can slip on south. If'n you don't want a share of the gains for your work 'cause you'd feel queasy 'bout it, that's your choosin'. You do what suits you." He paused again, letting me consider what he'd reasoned out.

"You're in a bad way, me boy. But, liken the Lord says, He'll help them that helps themselves. You gotta gain some leeway by tossen the Fort Frye crowd offen your scent. You ponder on that! Appears you could make out fine with what I done that time out along the mighty Mississip when I throw'd those damnable McDowds offen my trail. You remember that yarn I spun you, don't you? Sure you do. Ponder on it now. You use Cousin Hezekial over on the Muskingum any way you deem fit. Don't ask him for help in any way, just use him. I grant you, he be of our blood. But he don't honor allegiance to any, not even his Maker. He was in with your step-paw, but he'll jump onto the other foot an' uphold Lansford's river bunch and save his own neck. Nephew, you gotta get done what's goin' a-beggin' an' be as far upriver as you can by daybreak. Tomorray will be too late. Git what you need from the cabin an' my best hidey place, then git on with it. . . ."

A particle borne by the wind brushed my forehead. I blinked and Uncle Jeremiah vanished. But his disappearance didn't throw me off course; I followed orders. Without a moment's delay, I swiped the water from my brow and taken off for home, putting some straight up and down into my chilled frame.

Lord, how I loved Jeremiah, how I would always love him. All was not lost. His words warmed my soul and poured some grit and spunk into me. And he'd told how I could trick Lansford and his followers just as he'd fooled the McDowds, and with a little luck, make a clean getaway. It was a risky, dangerous scheme, but Uncle'd pulled it off and I'd take his suggestion and have my own stab at it.

I had no false hopes. By now Lansford had painted a mighty black picture of us Hannars, and the folks at Fort Frye likely judged me a fugitive, a man in rebellion against the lawful authority of the territory. At daybreak they'd come for me, rifles fully cocked and lynching nooses chafing their palms. It counted not I wasn't guilty of anything. Matthan Hannar either saved himself or perished.

Lansford planned a quick death at the end of a rope for me. But that wasn't to be, not if I had any say in things. Jeremiah and Stepfather had sacrificed themselves and spared my life.

Even if it cost the life they'd saved, their deaths wouldn't be for naught.

Chapter 4

By the time I reached the edge of our clearing and spied the cabin, sighting a spot where a scared lad could get warm and ease the hunger cramping his innards surely bolstered the soul.

But armed with an empty rifle and not desiring another Ballard fiasco, I didn't charge headlong for the door. I hunkered down and scouted in all directions with eye and ear.

The cabin appeared deserted. The unlatched shutter of the window banged with each gust of wind. Through the open door, the interior loomed black as the hold of a ship. No smoke came from the chimney. The hearth fire had burnt itself out.

While the cabin seemed deserted, still leery of a trap or ambush, I slow-footed around and checked the outbuildings first. What I found—open gates, an empty shed, empty pens—sat poorly with me. Gone was the horse team. Gone were the brindle cow and the sow pig. A single animal remained, the boar hog, flopped on his side in his pen, rainwater forging

runnels through the bristle on his flank, shot dead
under the near ear.

Lansford and the Ballards had probably led off the
horse team when carting the wounded colonel and
the bodies of Stepfather and Jeremiah to Fort Frye.
That I could understand. But loosing the cow and
the sow and slaying the boar smacked of spite,
and their callousness got my dander up. Driving and
ferrying the livestock from Fort Pitt had been a
toilsome chore, a task we'd undertaken establishing
the farm promised my mother if she came with us to
Ohio after marrying my Uncle John. I stood in the
mud, madder than a wet hen, furious that everything we'd done for her had amounted to nothing
whatsoever in the end.

I didn't rant and fuss overly long. The cold rain
had me shaking and shivering and a heap of discom-
fort gets a young man considering himself mighty
quick. Much too wet and miserable for prolonged
fussing over how things had turned out, I just
wanted to be warm and fed and gone from this place,
once a happy place, now one reeking of death and
shattered dreams.

I sidled over even with the near end of the cabin
and probed along the wall for Jeremiah's "look-see"
block. Back when we'd mortared twixt the logs,
Uncle had rigged a hunk of chinking we could
remove so as to look inside on the sly. I located the
loose block, wriggled it free, and stuck eye to black
hole. After a bit I made out the table and chairs, then
the hearth on the far side of the room. Nothing

there; no one waited in ambush. I trotted round front and ducked in the door.

The Ballard rifle landed on the table with a thump. I knelt before the hearth. A little digging with a poker fetched up a few embers from the ash pile with enough spark to fire a handful of oak shavings from the wood box. I added layers of cut wood, built a bright dancing flame, and soaked some heat into my bones. Once warmed through, I searched the room. Lansford and his hirelings had confiscated every gun and ounce of powder we Hannars owned, leaving me no means of defense unless I braved a tramp back out into the dreary night.

Out I tramped.

At the midpoint of the hill beyond the horse shed, a spring, long run dry, had carved a hole in a solid wall of stone. A towering slab of gray rock obscured the upper half of the hole; the bottom half Jeremiah had cleverly blocked with small boulders, denying passage to nosey snakes and varmints. Roll the boulders aside, scrunch down and worm your way under the slab overhang, and you popped up in a small cave—Uncle Jeremiah's "hidey place." On a ledge near the ceiling rested his possible sack, a smallish lead box filled with gunpowder and, wrapped in a buffalo hide, his Pennsylvania long rifle, necessaries secreted in the event the redskins burned the cabin while we were off running our trap line. I squirmed them through the opening one at a time, wedged the lead box under one arm, hefted the sack and bundled rifle, and beelined for the warmth of the hearth fire.

The possible sack—a military issue haversack—showed stout construction, being triple-stitched and deep-pouched. The sack contained most all the gear a trailing man needed for a long, bad-weathered journey. I spread the gear out on the table, recalling as I did my favorite of Jeremiah's many tales, the story Uncle told the evening he'd readied the haversack for storage in the cave.

"Always be prepared, anywheres, anytime, an' I say again, anytime," he'd started. "Why, I knowed a trapper, name of Caleb Passwater, foolish enough he let himself be bushwhacked answerin' the morning call of nature. There he be, smack in the open, ringed by green ivy an' yeller wildflowers, gun at the off hand, breeches bunched down round his ankle-bones, eyeballs pinched shut with the strain of it all. Can't you just see him, presentin' the whitest an' roundest an' easiest target in all God's realm? T'warn't no way that red devil Injun sneakin' up on our camp could pass over that pearl of a chance for annoyin' his most hated enemy. He strung an arrow, let fly . . . an' his shaft flew true.

"Believe you me, Caleb's bellers of pure hurt brung the rest of us on the run an' we saved his scalp. But I tell you, he was truly mortified at takin' an arrow in his most tenderest spot. An' us being an ornery bunch, we didn't comfort him maybe like we should've. You see, whilst we dug into his bare rump after that arrow with a knife by the fire, each of us took a whirl at bestin' the others in assurin' Caleb how handsome that arrow shaft stickin' out of him was.

"Now Caleb didn't die from the cuttin' we done on him. But that arrowhead chewed such a hole in the right ham of his backside he felt a heady pang of pain ever' time he taken a step for weeks. An' though we went out together in the mornin' from then on, with one of us standin' guard, Caleb wouldn't perform lessen he was jaw to jaw with his protector. He'd had all the funnin' he could bear.

"Thus, me lad, don't ever deny preparation ain't the savin' grace of all of us. A speck of time spent findin' a more woodsified spot and Caleb would've spared himself a bottomful of torment and embarrassment."

I laughed aloud. Never would I meet another man like Uncle Jeremiah. He'd never preached. He'd trained with his yarns and his ways. And true as his words, he'd stuffed the haversack with everything from powder horn and whetstone to glass vials of sassafras root, salt, and bear oil. He'd even included his old naval spyglass.

Jeremiah's long rifle slid easily from the roll of the buffalo hide. A star and the letters *J. H.*, made of dull metal, decorated the maple stock opposite the patch box. Thimbles secured the ramrod along the bottom of the barrel. The gun was in prime firing condition, lock mechanism well oiled, flint shiny and unused.

The glossy black grains of powder in the lead box felt tinder-dry at the touch of a finger. I poured the powder horn full, swabbed, loaded, and balled the long rifle, likewise the Ballard gun. That finished, I scaled the wall ladder. Jeremiah's sea chest was a shadowy lump in a dim corner of the loft. I'd never nibbed in it before, but I had no choice now. A flip of two metal hasps freed the lid. The Ballards hadn't disturbed its contents and beneath an old greatcoat nestled Uncle's second hatchet and sheathed skinning knife, both aged, passable if sharpened well. I took both hatchet and knife, and though unaware Jeremiah possessed a fine heavy old greatcoat, particularly one he never wore, I helped myself a second time.

Fully armed again, I barred the door and stripped, drying hunting frock, shirt, breeches, and moccasins over chairs before the fire. In the meantime the hunger cramping my innards needed tending. Our larder was bare of meat, but mealed corn, water, and poor flour kneaded into dollops of johnnycake and cooked at the hearth in a spider skillet greased with animal fat wasn't bad fare. The fat bubbled and spit in the iron pan, flattening and turning the doughy globs golden brown, letting off a mouth-watering smell. I gulped the first batch straight from the pan while mixing more batter, and fried and feasted till my gullet couldn't hold another morsel. Those corn cakes tasted right fine. I fried up some extra for the trail.

Full of belly and drier than the skin on a snake, I soon found my head nodding. I shook myself awake. I would pay dearly come the morning if I tarried and dozed off. I sacked up the last of the johnnycakes and fair jumped into my clothes.

Final preparations went smoothly at first. I dumped oak shavings from the wood box into the bottom of the haversack, repacked Jeremiah's gear, and lashed the emptied buffalo hide to the underside of the heavy pouch. With these finishing touches I was well fed, armed, supplied, and ready for action.

But danged if long about there I didn't slide within a whisker of throwing my life away. Strange as it may sound at first, what unleashed my feelings and brought me down on my knees again, more broken-hearted than ever, was the greatcoat from Jeremiah's sea chest. I failed to recognize the coat till I was putting it on. The recognition, when it came, dropped my jaw open. The coat wasn't Jeremiah's, nor was it Stepfather's.

It belonged to my father: Luke Hannar.

Taken aback, stunned at discovering something I'd believed lost forever, faster than a snap of the fingers I remembered my father and how he looked the first time I'd seen him in the greatcoat. Ten years ago to the month, in January of 17 and 82, Luke Hannar had marched home across the Alleghenies after fighting in the ranks against the redcoats and the Hessians. In the doorway that blustery afternoon he looked bigger in the long coat with the wide belt and giant pockets than the mountains he'd crossed on the trip home. And when he swept Mother off her feet and kissed her, I loved him so much I dreamt that very night of growing up just like him—a soldier tall enough to wear the greatcoat, a coat bigger than most other men.

Oh, how I wanted the greatcoat for my very own. If a boy could wear that awesome garment, he was growed. Like his father, he was a man.

I nagged and nagged and eventually Father agreed the coat would be mine the year my body matched the size of it. From that date forward, on the anniversary of his homecoming, I donned the coat and we measured my progress in narrowing the huge gap between the garment's vast bulk and my skinny bones. The annual measuring always meant great hilarity and fun, as anticipated by my family as the observance of birthdays.

The boyish dream of owning the coat became a part of me, heart and soul, till Father's death in a boat yard bawl at Fort Pitt shattered it forever. The seeming unfairness of his death enraged me. I cast the greatcoat amongst the ruts of the wagon road outside our cabin, stomped it deep into the rich black mud, and ran off. I hid and bawled all night, ignoring the beseeching calls of Jeremiah and Mother. Finally, hungry and cried out, I sneaked home at dawn and discovered someone had retrieved Father's coat from the sloppy roadbed. Neither Mother nor Jeremiah offered an explanation, and I'd been bull-stubborn and never asked about the muddied coat. I realized now, this night many years later, ever patient Jeremiah had retrieved the overcoat, saying nothing. He'd stowed it away in his sea chest for a later day.

The rush of memory blurred my eyes with tears, and shamed by the weakness gripping me, I thrust my arms into the sleeves of the coat. Big no more, the once huge garment fit perfectly. I moaned and the tears began flowing in earnest. At last I matched Father's greatcoat, and no one who cared was with me. All who'd loved me—Father, Mother, Stepfather—were dead and gone. A wave of wishful longing for times past and loved ones lost washed over me and I fell on my knees, sobbing, driven down by unbearable loneliness and sorrow.

The Lord Almighty must save his most precious gifts for when we are truly desperate. Leastways, I have no better explanation for what happened next. I mean I was on my knees, torn apart by personal agonies, unable to get on my feet and do something—anything—while it still mattered. Yet, at the very depths of my anguish, as I contemplated the surrender of all hope, somehow I scavenged up the courage to gather my ravaged feelings together and rekindle the determination not to die at the hands of a Van Hove mob bent on wrongful vengeance.

Anyone else may think as they like. I know one moment I lacked the courage I so desperately needed, the next I found it deep inside my soul. And just one *being* could have gifted me with such courage. After all, no one else shared the cabin with me that bleak night.

On the crude planks of the cabin floor, I let off the wailing and sniffling and gave myself a tongue-

lashing. I was sick of crying and sick of being afraid.
Tired and disheartened I might be, helpless and
without hope surely not. I set my jaw and vowed I'd
never again be brought to my knees. Never again
would boyish dreams, wishful longings, or hurtful
sufferings tear me apart. Henceforth, the Lord will-
ing, Matthan Hannar would stand tall like his
father and Uncle Jeremiah, strong and courageous,
prey for neither weakness nor unmanliness.

With that sobering vow I rose, thumbed the tears
from my eyes, and looped the harness of the haversack over my shoulders. On waist belt I strung knife,
shot pouch, powder horn, and hatchet. Into coat
pockets went the balance of my gear: fur cap, muffler, mittens, and tying thongs. I crammed a flat-
brimmed hat of Stepfather's on my head and filled
either hand with Jeremiah's long rifle and the Ballard gun.

I challenged my newly wrought courage before
dousing the fire, risking a final glance about the
cabin. From the mantle of the hearth dangled the
smoking tongs Jeremiah used to touch live coals to
the tobacco packed in his sea nymph pipe. Mother's
dusty spinning wheel sat nearby. The candle mold
she'd treasured lay on the sideboard. On the farthest
of the wooden pegs rowing the wall hung her shawl,
such a warm reminder of her we'd not dared dispose
of it. Catching my eye last was the leather-bound
tablet in which I recorded the days and months and
remarks on the Hannar family. That I couldn't part
with. I made room for the diary in a coat pocket.

Departure from the cabin wrenched my heart. But my eyes were dry and my head up. I snugged the door shut and headed for Cousin Hezekial's trading post on the Muskingum. My future, whatever was left of it, would be played out in a setting of my choosing with the advantage of surprise on my side for a change.

Come the devil or high water, I would prove myself man enough to wear Father's greatcoat.

Chapter 5

The moonless night favored an overland trek with little risk of detection. A traveler could see just close at hand, a few rods at best. The steady rain altered constantly with the wind, first pattering lightly on the blanket of dead leaves carpeting the floor of the forest, then drumming heavily on the same lifeless remnants of months gone by. Bare and open ground turned sticky as mushed corn. Backwoodsmen were wary of such January storms. They ushered in unseasonal thaws, then rapidly gave way before seasonal freezes of great duration. It might well be raving cold and snowing by noon tomorrow.

The raw, dank night suited me fine. Settlers and their dogs would stay indoors, bequeathing the foul darkness to the desperate few such as I who either braved the elements or risked death by remaining where they were. And the warming weather would choke the Muskingum River Valley with a soupy fog before sunrise, a fog that would last for hours and hinder those hunting me with hanging rope in hand.

I followed the bank of Wolf Creek downstream till

I reached Colonel Van Hove's grist mill. Beside the unmanned two-story mill the rising waters of the creek rippled over a solid limestone bottom. I slogged across to the far bank and loped into the woods, angling away from the stream. Wolf Creek coursed behind me and mated with its south branch, curved short of Waterford, then snaked around northward before turning again and emptying into the Muskingum. The beaten path bordering the stream from the mill to Waterford would've been a less strenuous route, but I couldn't be certain all the villagers had indeed crossed the Muskingum and taken shelter behind the Fort Frye palisade.

A mile of hard plodding found me at the south branch of Wolf Creek. I forded, stepping from rock to rock, and paused, getting my wind and my bearings. The terrain straight ahead roughened, climbing and steepening, breaking into rows of tall hills separated by deep ravines and gullies. Over left a couple of miles sat Waterford. Beyond the town site a ridge butted up against the Muskingum, and on the far bank, facing the far end of the ridge, was Fort Frye. Off right sprawled unsettled country. Being doubly safe, I circled right before quartering eastward toward the river, seeking Cousin Hezekial's trading post on the near bank of the Muskingum below Waterford.

I planned on stealing Hezekial's keelboat and steering it downriver a fair ways, after which I would abandon the keelboat in mid-river for a skiff and row back upriver between Fort Frye and Waterford, then come ashore at the mouth of Wolf Creek. A dangerous, ambitious scheme, I concede. But I'd none better. It'd worked for Uncle Jeremiah years ago out on the Mississippi. And if carried off, it would bless me with a lengthy head start into Injun country while my pursuers rushed after the empty keelboat. It mattered little if Lansford's boys learned later they'd been hoodwinked. They wouldn't trail me upriver any great distance—they feared the redskins too much for that.

Sheerly by happenstance, I stumbled abreast the trading post shortly after midnight. I would've wandered past that sizable structure in the dark if not for Hezekial's keelboat. I eared the creaks and groans of the moored vessel's hull a scant step before bumping into the railing of the catwalk that descended the bank to the ship's dock. More startled than hurt, I dropped on one knee, looking and listening, alert as a fox stalking a guarded henhouse.

The wind rattled brittle leaves on a few tree branches. Raindrops dappled the surface of the mud puddle edging the catwalk. The keelboat nudged the dock when the current of the river ebbed. Otherwise, the black night matched a silent prayer at a church meeting.

The post building, sixty yards up the slope from the catwalk, couldn't be seen from the riverbank. An approach from downwind and the backside seemed in order. I'd been a fugitive for less than a day, but I reasoned like one already. Most every fugitive, if he

cherished remaining free and unfettered, showed a
distaste for rapping on the front door if a dwelling's
owners hadn't already made known their sentiments regarding his outlawed station in life. For all
I knew, if Hezekial or one of his cohorts was to home,
either might just as leave shoot me as shake my
hand. A dead Matthan Hannar couldn't hardly re-
veal the past associations of his shirttail cousin with
that infamous Indian trader, Abel Stillwagon, could
he now!

I backtracked a hundred yards and zigzagged
uphill through the rock outcroppings littering the
slope amongst the sparse timber. The rain slackened, becoming a drizzle. I identified the pitch of the
post roof against the slightly lightened skyline, and
the wind teased my nostrils with the pungent odor of
wood smoke. I scurried for the leeward portion of the
nearest tree trunk.

Whorls of smoke slipped downwind. They came
from a steady, tended fire.

Someone was to home.

Straight out I eliminated my cousin. Though he
went by the name Parsons and didn't brag of his
blood ties with us Hannars, Hezekial, a devious
rascal, maintained a paid spy at Fort Frye and he
would be across the river at Lansford's meeting,
allaying any possible hint he had had a hand in the
Indian dealings with Stepfather and Stillwagon. In
his absence, guarding the post would undoubtedly
be Toby, his half-black, half-red servant and roust-
about. A superstitious misfit, the breed insisted

demons and evil spirits roved the night. He'd hide
indoors till dawn or till Hezekial returned from Fort
Frye. His presence didn't discourage me any; I'd a
thing needed doing and it couldn't be done cowering
back of a tree.

First off, was Toby ensconced behind barricaded
doors? My scheme required access to the post. If
Toby needed overpowering, even shooting to get in,
so be it. But no need for foolhardiness. Toby being a
powerfully built man, I preferred surprising him
and sparing both of us undue grief.

Beams of light winked between the boards of the
shutter covering the closest window. I padded for
that opening, cursing softly when my feet rustled
leaves heaped back under the protecting eave of the
roof by the wind. I needn't have worried. I peeked
through the largest of the cracks in the shutter and
located Toby. The breed lay sprawled on his chest
before the fire, an overturned whiskey jug at his hip.
He'd seemingly partaken of too much liquid courage
warding off his nocturnal demons and spirits. He
snored louder than a pit saw biting into dry wood.

I couldn't help grinning. Perhaps in his drunken-
ness Toby had neglected the minding of the doors.
The doors could be seen from my vantage point and,
sure enough, the back door was shut and barred but
the front, crossbar leaning against the jam, was ajar.
His carelessness provided an opportunity for gaining the upper hand without a struggle.

At the rear of the post I stashed the long rifle and
the haversack atop the woodpile there. If Toby

awakened, he must see only the Ballard gun. If he
saw the long rifle and the pack and later learned
they weren't found downriver on the keelboat, he
might question their absence and expose Matthan
Hannar's diversion for what it was—a clever decep-
tion. On the other hand, if I didn't stub my toe, come
morning all could easily accept things as I wanted.

If perchance there was a tussle with Toby, a
misfire of the Ballard gun couldn't be chanced. By
the light of the shutter crack I pocketed the lock
cover from Joseph's rifle and thumbed open the
frizzen of the lock. A puff of breath blew the powder
from the firing pan, and a flick with a vent pick
reamed the touchhole clear. Once I'd reprimed the
pan with fresh powder, I crept past the front corner
of the post and eased out into the commons yard.

The rattle of a chain—and only that warned me.

I jumped back, shielding my face with the Ballard
rifle. Fangs snapped an inch from my arm, a hollow
clicking that sent spidery fingers of fear racing down
my spine.

The mastiff, a huge brute of a dog, hung sus-
pended in midair, stopped short at the end of his
chain. The abrupt halt jolted the breath from him,
and I felt the warmth of it on my hands. I slashed at
the beast with the rifle. The heavy barrel caught
him below the ear, knocking him senseless. He
landed with a solid thud, legs twitching, mouth
slobbering.

I yanked a handful of tying thongs from the pocket
of the greatcoat, tied those massive jaws, then bound

his legs. Chest heaving, hands quaking, I sat on my haunches staring at the mastiff. Barrel-chested, long of limb, he had paws wider than my palms. I hated the beast for almost tearing my arm off. But admiration warmed me too. No bark or growl'd betrayed him. A little less anxious and he would've nailed me proper.

The mastiff regained his senses, tested the deer-hide thongs, found them too strong for breaking and accepted his fate, not wasting himself on a hopeless endeavor. A smart beast. I scooped up the rifle and headed for the front door of the trading post.

A few paces from the stoop I heard Toby's grating snores. I gently shoved the door open. He hadn't budged. On his shirtless body, muscle bulged like coiled rope. His kinky hair shone in the firelight. I crept near and jabbed him sharply in the ribs with the muzzle of the Ballard gun.

Toby's forehead being flush with the floor, just his right eye could be observed. The eye popped open, widened in alarm, widened more, and widened yet again. I thought the yellow orb would burst from the socket.

I couldn't rightly blame him. The sodden brim of my hat sagged past my nose. A turned-up coat collar veiled my ears, throat, and mouth. The greatcoat teemed with thorns, stickers, and thistle needles from the night march. I appeared a sightless, god-less demon. Who else but a demon of the dark, the thing the poor devil feared the most, could sneak into the post past his watchdog, that huge mastiff, without being chewed apart?

I'll say this much for Toby, his dismay didn't last long. The breed casually lowered the lid of his eye, feigning another passing out spell . . . and tricked me pure and simple.

With the swiftness of a striking snake, he clamped the barrel of my rifle with one hand, sprang upward, and stabbed at my belly with a knife. I sucked in my gut and twisted sideways. The liquor in him spared me. It ruined his aim. The knife missed my belly and lodged harmlessly in the front flap of the greatcoat. For an instant Toby was as defenseless as the mastiff at the end of the chain. I fisted my hand, swung backhanded, and connected with the very point of his chin, landing a lucky, brutal punch.

Torn from his feet by the force of the blow, Toby twisted about and smashed face first against the plank floor, arched his back, and went limp. A trickle of bright red blood seeped from under his head.

I angrily ripped the knife from the flap of the greatcoat, pitched the weapon into the fire, and trussed Toby's hands so tightly the thongs gouged the skin of his wrists. I finished the tying and my anger cooled. Since the breed couldn't resist, abusing him wasn't proper. I was really angry with myself anyway. Letting the mastiff almost tear an arm off could be overlooked; no watchdog had been at the post on previous visits. The tussle with Toby was a horse of a different color. Instead of handling his capture like a man with something more than a smattering of brains, I'd gloated over catching him in a drunken stupor and fallen for a simple ruse, the kind of silly stupid mistake that'd killed far better men than I.

Loosening his bindings a tad, I raised Toby's head. His smashed and bruised face was an awful visage, but he breathed evenly. If Hezekial didn't shoot him for swilling corn liquor and not guarding the post, he'd live. I gingerly lowered his head cheek side down.

The trading post secured, I got cracking. It was late and Hezekial or some of his henchmen might show suddenlike in the doorway and spoil my getaway.

Uncle Jeremiah always said, "When you're tricken a fella, don't make it hard on him. Shake out a scent any dumb hound can follow without prowlin' all over." I would lay a smelly scent, one I trusted would lead my pursuers in the wrong direction, with a letter to Hezekial. A missive affirming Hezekial's purported innocence of trading with the Indians would gladden his devious soul. He'd hustle before Lansford Van Hove, present written evidence I'd robbed his post and taken off with his keelboat, and the downriver chase would be on.

Some pilfering preceded the letter writing. To spice my scheme I would discard on the keelboat the Ballard gun and a cache of stolen supplies. When the boys flagged down the keelboat and turned up no sign I'd reached the bank, my leavings might convince them I'd fallen overboard and drowned, since a

fleeing man never willingly parted with his necessaries. A long shot, but worth the effort.

The thievery took no time atall. Hezekial's stock of
goods ranged from guns, pigs of lead, traps, and tools
to flitches of bacon and lidded tubs of salt pork, all
stacked or shelved the length of the front wall.
Behind the counter rested his desk and mounds of
deer, beaver, and otter pelts. The mounds were low,
the pelts few in number. The good trapping season
had begun, but the redskin troubles would hamper
the catch all winter. Even someone no smarter than
me appreciated why Hezekial had thrown in with
Abel Stillwagon: one prosperous exchange with the
dreaded Ohio Indians would offset an otherwise
meager year for a fur trader.

I piled the supplies collected from about the room on
the largest of the deerhides, drew up the edges, and
secured the cumbersome bale with a piece of rope.
Then I wrote the letter. A sheet of parchment from
Hezekial's ledger book provided paper; a Betty lamp,
rag wick fired at the hearth, gave forth light enough;
an inkstand and quill pen I snitched from the desk.

Elbows planted on the counter, greasy smoke from
the lamp stinging my eyes, I penned the most
important message of my young life:

Mr. Parsons
    I taken salt pork, bacon, tea, traps, lead, and
    bullet mold. Sorry you be hurt by troubles no
    maken of your'en.
                                        M. Hannar

I read the letter twice over. Not naming Hezekial a relative was deliberate. Many folks swore by the old saw—dogs sleeping together bred the same fleas—and Hezekial might hesitate in sharing the letter with Lansford if it revealed his blood kinship with the Hannars. I positioned the sheet of parchment, weighted down with the inkstand, in the center of Hezekial's desk.

The knots binding Toby were still plenty taut. The breed snored peacefully again. I spread a coarse blanket over him, lugged the deerhide bale and the Ballard rifle outside, recovered the long rifle and the haversack from the woodpile, then hiked downhill for the river, staggering a little under the load of it all.

Make no mistake, I'd been lucky journeying overland at night without a serious fall, even luckier in escaping unscathed the fangs of the mastiff and Toby's blade. And my ordeal was far from over. The most demanding segment of my scheme remained undone, but I'd no other choice except plow through to the end. After the crime I'd just committed, nothing short of a miracle would change the opinion of the Fort Frye settlers that Matthan Hannar was decidedly lacking in saintly qualities.

Maybe I'd climbed in on my own rather than at the bidding of the Ballards as before, but I'd slid back in that box with no lid.

Chapter 6

The ending of the night rain thinned the clouds shrouding the moon, and I descended the steps of the catwalk to the boat dock without incident. At the bottom of the steps I wrapped three flitches of bacon and a few traps from the deerhide bale in my buffalo hide. The meat wrapped in the hide and the johnny-cakes in the haversack would sustain me till I could trap for my vittles. Any man with a grain of respect for the Injuns did little shooting when traveling alone in their territory.

The size of the keelboat, moored fore and aft with thick rope hawsers, awed an upcreeker like me. Forty feet long, eight feet in beam, the vessel was short of bow and stern. A cargo box six feet high covered the whole of its middle. A narrow cleated walkway ran all around the gunwales for footing for the poling crew, and seats for rowers filled the bow. A long oar pivoted atop a steering stoop in the stern served as the main means of steerage. The keelboat dwarfed the dock, glistening with moisture in the feeble light.

I suppose a fair-to-middlin' worshiper of the Almighty should've been aghast he was considering the theft of such an enormously valuable piece of property. Be that as it may, I didn't feel guilty in the least. Desperation will drive a beleaguered man to the most sinful of deeds in the hope he can avert his own extinction.

Tied from an eyebolt in the railing at the keelboat's stern floated a sharp-prowed skiff, one of two Hezekial owned. He seldom had need for both on a given night, and I'd trusted one would be available. I was still relieved to see it. Without the rowboat my scheme had no more consequence than a flash in the pan of a long rifle.

Maneuvering the keelboat from the dock took a tad of cleverness. I stowed my gear at the foot of the steering oar. Next I chopped through the fore mooring line with my hatchet. The current pushed the bow out and away from the dock, and I hotfooted along the cleated walkway for the mooring hawser in the stern, watched the ship come about and point downriver, then cut the aft line. The keelboat drifted clear of the dock pretty as you please.

The Muskingum was on the rise after the rain and the keelboat picked up speed fast. With no one at the helm the ship might run aground. But the rising water would likely warp her free and wash her on downstream toward Marietta. The ship drew no more than two feet of water and could withstand a lot of tossing about without sinking. Unless severely holed, she would still be afloat at dawn.

Discarding the Ballard gun and the bale of stolen supplies by the steering oar, I tugged the skiff in close and handed the long rifle and the haversack down into it. The bobbing rowboat seemed about the size of an acorn. I screwed up my courage and levered my legs over the stern of the keelboat. So far, so good. But when I reached up from the skiff and untied the tow rope, all hell broke loose.

The freed skiff lost way and slipped astern so quickly it swept the legs from under me. I frantically latched onto the railing of the keelboat with both hands. But the skiff continued to lose way, stretching me out like a deerskin staked out for drying. The sorriest excuse for a bridge ever, feet dangling in the skiff, fingers locked in a death grip on the keelboat railing, I watched pop-eyed the steady growth of a horrifying expanse of black water beneath my belly.

Fortunately, luck stuck with me. Someway my feet wedged together in the skiff's sharp prow and I humped my body and pulled with my arms. Amazingly, my feet and shinbones didn't split asunder at the ankles. Nor did I lose my handhold. I gradually closed the yawning space separating the two crafts, sweating mightily.

But I couldn't let it go at that, that wasn't my youngish style. Once on my feet again in the skiff, I got downright bold, too bold. I spun away from the railing . . . and lost my balance. With all the grace of a rock, I tumbled headfirst into the bottom of the skiff, whanging my noggin on the center seat. This fit of heedless abandon earned me a knot on the skull that thumped for a week. Thoroughly disgusted, I dipped the oars into the water and started rowing with long, even strokes. The misty gloom swallowed the keelboat in nothing flat.

Anyone familiar with boats knows that you sit backwards when rowing a skiff. Lest care be taken, one can wander hither and yon all over a river at night, wasting time and strength. At night you stick tight along the bank, and the black line of trees fringing the shore will set your course. And by sticking in the shallower waters along the shore, an upstream rower avoids the main force of the downstream current, saving more time and strength. Into the bank I went.

Ahead waited a straight span of water, a sharp left bend, a second spurt of straight rowing past Fort Frye, followed by a sharp right bend, then the final run past Waterford to a landing above the mouth of Wolf Creek.

My worst fright of the night occurred a short jaunt round that first bend, the sharp left. There the Muskingum had undercut its bank and felled a mammoth old sycamore. The underside of the toppled tree lay buried in the mud of the riverbed with a host of topside branches protruding above the waterline. The protruding branches were treacherous as a cordon of spears, and I rowed the skiff right into the middle of them.

Having drifted wide rounding the bend, I was bent forward sweeping fast with the oars for the shallows when something snatched the hat from my head.

Before I could respond to this ominous hint of impending trouble, a second branch jarred my elbow, a third snagged my coat collar, and the skiff rammed a submerged limb and stopped dead in the water, almost unseating me.

I hadn't any more fastened a hand on a wet slippery branch, staying the skiff, and a voice said, "Donna fret 'bout your houn', Mr. Parsons. We'll heel him home hale and hearty after the hunt."

By all that was holy—there could be no mistake— that was the voice of Timothy Ballard! And Mr. Parsons? None other than my shirttail cousin, Hezekial.

You've heard how the hair on your neck can stand on end if a lad be frightened badly enough. My fright had to be of a rare and monumental nature because every hair on my lanky frame lifted clean from the hide. I even feared they would hear the knot on my skull thumping, which sounded just then inside my head like the high notes of a hunting horn.

They had me. They couldn't miss me. Their skiff slipped along no more than the length of a packhorse from the outermost branch of the deadfall, and while the low fog forming on the surface of the river concealed their boat, the opposite was true of their hats, shoulders, and beards: these could be seen with no problem atall. I had to be plain as a bullfrog trapped in the glow of a gigger's lantern.

"I'll not fret, Timothy. I trust you and the others will have that young hellion Matthan noosed high by noon today."

"That we will, sir! That we will!"

They didn't see me. And they didn't because of a fault common to all hunters of man and beast at one time or another: not expecting their quarry to be hung up in the shadowy limbs of the deadfall, they weren't looking for me. They glided by in the thickening fog, none the wiser.

I rested my forehead on my arm, gladly granting the two of them time to glide out of earshot before the breath departed me in one big relieved *whoosh*! Being so frightened a hunter couldn't breathe didn't always result in an unmanly experience after all. If I'd rooted in the bottom of the skiff for the long rifle, they'd have seen me or heard me and taken me like Timothy said earlier, ". . . easy as pickin' a hickory nut offen the ground."

Thank the Lord I'd heeded Jeremiah's advice. Uncle had been right in his predictions. With no solid evidence against me personally, my neighbors had declared the youngest of the Hannars a fugitive and organized themselves to track me down.

Their faulty judgment taught a lesson I wouldn't soon forget. A man needn't be guilty when incurring the wrath of others; the mere appearance of guilt can cause him to be unjustly wronged and treated as if he'd committed the most dastardly of crimes. It didn't count for anything you'd lived ten and nine years as I had without seriously offending another man or professing greed or a mean nature. Whether I liked it or not, it was the lynching rope or the land of the redskins for Matthan Hannar.

Well, I didn't like it. I dug hat from stern, hove the skiff clear of the branches of the deadfall, and resumed my upriver voyage, hell-bent once again on denying Lansford Van Hove the pleasure of killing off the last of the Hannars.

Once past Fort Frye on the opposite shore, I rowed about the right bend in the Muskingum above the stockade and encountered new difficulties. The long session at the oars gradually devoured my waning strength and with it, my determination. My blistered hands stiffened like claws. A searing pain rampaged through my arms and down my back into my legs. Twice I ducked my head in the water, fighting off exhaustion. Every sweep of the oars became sheer torture. I thought of that preacher who'd spoken at Sunday meetings during our year at Fort Pitt. How he'd lied! A fate worse than the fiery pits of damnation that young Bible-thumper lavishly depicted in his sermons *could* befall a man: he could be condemned to a long siege of rowing on a rising river surrounded by swirling gray fog. For all I knew, Satan himself had been birthed on the Muskingum in a skiff.

My strength shot, the pain grew intolerable. Enough was enough. Short of my planned landing beyond Wolf Creek, I headed into the bank.

A dog barked! Other hounds chimed in. A din of howling and growling swelled along the waterway. I halted the rowboat and held a steady position with light strokes of the oars. The dogs, I soon realized, hadn't spotted the boat in the dense fog. They heard the squeaky rasp of the oars in their locks.

Whose dogs?

A fuzzy shaft of yellow light pierced the cloying fog. "Shet up, you addle-brained bunch of useless curs! Shet up or Zed and me will whup the stuffin's out of ya! Ain't no one out there on a night like this'un!"

A door slammed, blocking off the shaft of fuzzy light. The pack reluctantly obeyed their master. The howling and growling softened, then subsided altogether.

Zed?

Of course, Zed Shaw! The skiff fronted the Shaw cabin. They farmed a parcel of bottomland within yards of the mouth of Wolf Creek, and old man Shaw, too cantankerous to fort up and tolerate the leadership of Colonel Van Hove, headed the clan. A widower, he shared the cabin with his twin sons, Zed and Zeb, both ornery as ring-tailed coons, and Zelda, a skinny unmarried daughter. Zelda wore long pants, straddled a horse like a man, talked with birds, and cussed an unladylike blue streak whenever the mood hit her. It was nearing dawn and that feisty lot was up early, breakfasting before a roaring fire.

What it came down to, lest Matthan Hannar craved a nose-to-nose meeting with the Shaw hounds, he'd better pick another landing site. A downriver landing meant sneaking around behind the dogs on foot. Nothing else beat a landing beyond

Wolf Creek, which put the stream between me and the snarling pack. Much as I hated it, I pointed the skiff upriver, gritted my teeth, and laid into the oars for one final go-round.

The Shaw hounds proved doggone inspirational. I overcame my pain and not only surpassed the mouth of Wolf Creek, but rowed another half mile before calling it quits.

Guiding the skiff into shore, I boated the oars and cast the iron ball attached to the anchor rope over a tree root. Then, crampy legs splayed wide for balance, I unloaded the long rifle and haversack. The bank lifted too high there for hauling the skiff into the trees. I whacked a gaping hole in its bottom with my hatchet and scrambled ashore. Water bubbled and gurgled into the skiff. It filled with water and sank from sight. I picked up the iron ball with both hands and from a crouch threw it underhanded as far out over the water as I could. The ball hit with a mighty splash and sank instantly, jerking the anchor rope under with it.

That completed my diversion. Now I had to wind my way through miles of territory controlled by wild savages, locate the rendezvous site, then await the arrival of Abel Stillwagon, a scoundrel as yet unawares he had a new partner . . . and who might not want one.

Good thing I was a praying man.

Chapter 7

How fine it would've been to dawdle awhile, strike a fire and ease wearied limbs and blistered hands and throbbing head.

I didn't.

I couldn't.

Oh, the missing keelboat and the letter on Hezekial's desk would lure the lynch mob into a fruitless quest downriver, of that I'd no doubts. Sometime later this very morning they'd come upon the drifting keelboat, find aboard only the Ballard gun and the stolen supplies, and scour the riverbanks close about. After unearthing no sign anyone had gone ashore they'd reckon their prey had either drowned or lighted out in the skiff, then search downriver past where the Muskingum joined the wide Ohio at Marietta, once more fetching up no trace of their quarry. At that juncture a confounded Lansford Van Hove would suppose Matthan Hannar dead or beyond his immediate reach in the skiff, and with the entire day wasted, have little choice except lead his jaded search party home to Fort Frye.

Knowing that, a brasher, less cautious lad might've dawdled in front of a fire at least through the forenoon. But the elder Van Hove proved a nagging worry. The colonel, in all likelihood, had withstood Jeremiah's winging shot, and even bedridden and hurting, the old bull still commanded the fort. He might well order an upriver search and spoil my diversion. The colonel lacked Lansford's rash manner and gullibility. He might believe Jeremiah Hannar's nephew clever enough to hoodwink his son and flee upriver for Indian territory. Thus, weariness and blisters and thumping head aside, I needed to lay tracks while the Fort Frye crowd wasted the day. I slung the haversack onto my back, shouldered the long rifle, and taken out of there upriver in a shambling, stumbling gait.

Heavy brush drenched from the night rain flanked the Muskingum. Every clump shed showers of water at the slightest touch. Thick tendrils of fog, ghostly white in the murky light of winter dawn, danced and twisted before the morning breeze. A few lurching steps and I couldn't see beyond the tip of my nose. All told, the wet choking brush, dim light, and dancing fog made the river bottom a right eerie, nightmarish place at daybreak.

Somewhere nearby dead reeds crackled and snapped as some biggish creature switched positions in rapid bounds. Never did I determine whether the noisemaker had two legs or four legs. An icy twinge of panic laid hold of me and in a whipstitch I feared a redskin waited behind every clump of brush, tomahawk poised for the death blow. Panic sprouted a will of their own in my feet, which suddenly craved to be elsewheres—fast—and I knuckled under to their silly craving, barging headlong into the heavy brush, pointed plumb away from the riverbank, headed for high ground and some seeing and breathing room.

Thank the Lord a long ridge of goodly height ran along to the Muskingum 'bout half mile back. Otherwise I might be a-running yet.

I barged and blundered and clawed pell-mell up the face of the ridge. Once on the crest of it, the fog dwindled to a shimmering haze, the underbush slackened, and I could gaze a fair distance round about. So much for imaginary redskins . . . nary a one could be spotted in any direction.

Winded by the steep climb and feeling decidedly foolish, I plopped down on the trunk of a handy deadfall. The panic ebbed and shame nearly gagged me. Where was that valiant lad who vowed on his knees just last night he'd forever be strong and courageous, prey neither to weakness nor unmanliness?

Rest assured, I'd meant that vow, every word. But nothing came from kidding oneself. Good intentions and broken vows cobbled the road bound for ruination and failure. I'd skimmed through a long desperate night on sheer luck and brute strength and hadn't learned a thing—a little fog and sudden noise had spooked me into an uphill charge that'd worn my legs to a frazzle.

I clucked my tongue in utter disgust.

It was high time I grew up. High time I thrust boyish foolishness behind me once and for all; high time the old noggin did more than anchor my hat. I was, after all, trapped betwixt a mighty big rock and a mighty hard place. Every step upriver widened my lead over Lansford and his mob, but even a gold coin had two sides: every step also led smack into outright Injun country. I could ill afford for the redskins—Shawnee, Delaware, or Ottawa—to fix eyes on me. Since I'd never traded with them as had Stepfather and Stillwagon, the red devils had scant reason for looking on Matthan Hannar with any special favor. White be white, and the only good white lad was a dead white lad where they were concerned. And when they didn't kill a man on sight, the Ohio Indians found particular delight in running an enemy down and torturing him to death. Cut it any way you please, a trek up the Muskingum in January of 17 and 92 was fraught with peril and danger, a task not to be taken lightly or gone about carelessly.

The rising winter sun, a yellow stain through the shimmering haze, brightened the eastern sky. It mattered not. I did as I shouldn't. I dawdled on the deadfall, weak-kneed and deathly tired, aching from heel to crown.

The longer I tarried, the more overwhelming seemed the tiredness and pain. I was too young that morning to fully appreciate an old truth—bodily miseries dwelled upon very long breed doubts and misgivings in a man about his being able to handle the task at hand, and once doubts and misgivings beset him, gumption and determination slip away powerfully quick. Believe you me, the doubts and misgivings that popped into my thumping head gnawed an awesome hole in my determination.

How could a scared lad who'd never journeyed into Injun territory with a fellow hunter, let alone by himself, expect to travel deep into such country and hide out till Abel Stillwagon arrived at the rendezvous site?

Wasn't it foolhardy and god-awful stupid to believe my best chance for survival was a successful rendezvous with Abel Stillwagon, the very scoundrel responsible for all my troubles?

What if the Shawnees pulled a double-cross, robbed him of his plunder, and left the big-nosed trader and his stiff-footed partner scalped and smoldering in a torture pit?

What if Stillwagon simply changed his plans and never showed?

Worse yet, what if Stillwagon showed, heard me out, then shot the last of the Hannars to still his tongue?

My head sagged. The doubts and worries seemed insurmountable. Lord forbid, even surrender at Fort Frye hardly appeared as poorly a choice as it had just last night.

I dawdled, and dawdled. My legs and feet after a while seemed somewhat better. But dallying and feeling sorry about everything, wasting precious time because I lacked sufficient gumption, blushed me with a heavy pang of guilt. My spirits hit rock bottom when I thought of how Jeremiah would look upon my dallying and doubting. Without any deliberation atall, I knew exactly what Uncle Jeremiah would say if he were present, could almost hear the words:

"Matthan, be you a sheep or be you a fox?"

Whenever anything had rattled my tree for no good reason, Uncle always spat out the same challenge like a hissing tomcat, eyes bright with a hard glint:

"Matthan, be you a sheep or be you a fox?"

Uncle claimed sooner or later all trailing men experienced the cold sweat of panic when properly spooked. What stood the test in the Ohio backcountry was how trailing men did for themselves after that clutch of cold terror came calling. Jeremiah maintained some hunters never determined whether they faced a real or a fancied danger. They barged and blundered about in a heedless fashion like sheep, creatures with such a dearth of good sense their favorite ploy when attacked was to stampede for the nearest spot of low ground and mill about, bleating haplessly while their attackers shredded the hide from them.

Contrariwise, unlike those whom terror converted

into sheep, other hunters, Uncle claimed, speared by the same stab of pure fright, kept their wits about them and likened themselves to the fox roused by a pack of hounds. True, the harried fox ran away as did the sheep. But unlike the sheep, the fox ran with a purpose. He galloped, then trotted, galloped, then trotted, husbanding his strength. He planned his escape route, always gaining ground on the barking hounds, not reckoning he was safe till their baying hadn't been heard for hours. Even then the wily fox deigned rest. He searched till he found a secure den, readying himself for a new run for his life before the next foe had been sighted or scented.

Jeremiah's challenge stuck in my mind.

"Matthan, be you a sheep or be you a fox?"

I pondered on it some. A sheep would go on barging and blundering about till the Fort Frye crowd caught up to him, then bleat haplessly for mercy before a hanging noose peeled the skin from his neck. Took all of the blink of an eye, it did, to see playing the sheep wouldn't wash for the nephew of Jeremiah Hannar.

Playing the fox appeared a much better bet. I knew the lay of the land thereabouts from trapping and salt gathering forays with Stepfather and Jeremiah. Eight miles or so over to the west, the Muskingum swept abruptly northward, then bent around in a ragged half circle and flowed southeast again past the bottom of the ridge upon which I now sat. A smart old fox would forego the bank of

the river and shortcut due west for where the
Muskingum made its abrupt northern turn, saving
many a step and many a mile. And a short hike after
the shortcut awaited a fine den—a cave with a
spring.

A hollow booming report echoed up the river
valley, snapping my head up. The long thunderous
rumble interrupted my pondering. It had to be the
signal cannon at Fort Frye. I listened closely.

A second report echoed up the Muskingum. Two
shots. An alert had been signaled.

Still I listened. One more report meant that
everyone—man, woman, and child—should seek
the safety of the Fort Frye palisade with all speed
possible. A fourth shot, however, would be most
revealing. Four signal firings meant only male bear-
ers of arms need answer the summons. And since the
next militia muster didn't occur for another two
days, four shots on this morning meant the search
for Matthan Hannar commenced shortly.

The third and fourth reports of the cannon followed at a measured pace. The final rumbling echo
answered squarely Uncle Jeremiah's challenge. The
fox surely had it over the sheep, now and forever.
Smell of wool fouled the nose anyway.

Maybe he was truly dead and gone, but Jeremiah's
prophecy yet held fast. His teachings had saved the
game for me one more time, pointing out the next
move. He would guide his nephew through "this here
silly fuss," just as he'd promised.

Without further babying of wilted legs and ouchy, blistered hands, I hitched feet beneath me and taken off westward down the ridge line. Just as any smart old fox would've.

Chapter 8

That shortcut proved a heady challenge for any wily old fox. It led across the upper reaches of a mean godforsaken hunk of backcountry where no game or hunting trails existed to ease passage. Timber on the brow of the ridge line felled by lightning and storm wind blocked the way time and again and had to be clumb over or gone around. Creeping mats of vine concealed countless tree roots and rocks, and I found the few open glens overgrown with spiny bushes and well-nigh impassable. I plugged ever onward, stride after jolting stride, stubbornly refusing any halt before regaining the river. Once off my feet, I'd sleep for hours. As with the smart fox, first a secure den, then victuals and rest.

The morning passed, an eternity of slow progress westward. The meager warmth of the winter sun melted the lingering haze from the upland, but lacked the heat for burning away the heavy lowland fog. From the ridge line the roiling sea of gray mist smothering the lowlands, white here, gray there, black further out, dazzled the mind and captured the eye. I was staring out over the top of it when I tripped on a tangle of vine and went sprawling in a nasty fall. Spitting dead leaves and bits of twig, I righted myself, pained and a smidgen wiser: blessed be the traveler who fixed his eyeballs on his moccasins and kept them there.

The fall hurt but spared a greater calamity. At midday, a quarter step beyond a cluster of scruffy box elm, the ridge line ended without an inkling atop a sheer cliff. If I'd been larking along then bewitched by the fog I would've sailed over the brink and splattered on the rocks down below like a gut-shot bird. It was still a near thing. I teetered on the cliff edge, one foot touching nothing more promising than thin air. Too tuckered out for anything fancy, I leaned back and sat down hard and quick. The stony rim of the cliff held my weight without breaking away, and I ended up perched on the very lip of the rim, legs hanging free and clear in the wind, clutching the precious Pennsylvania rifle against my chest.

It was an iffy, lofty perch, a real heart-pounder. I hung dead still for some long moments. The thought of those jagged rocks at the bottom of the cliff stiffened every bone. By and by, it came on me I was fairly well seated, not going anywheres soon, and I bent forward a hair and chanced a downward glance twixt my knees.

I'll never willingly hang on the rim of a cliff again feeling no more secure than a drop of sweat on the end of your nose. But on this occasion that downward glance at first certainly gladdened flagging spirits. Despite agonies to every bone and joint, despite a thumping knot on my skull, despite gnawing hunger and parching thirst, despite the narrow escape from a deadly plunge off the cliff face, I'd at least completed my cross-country shortcut as planned. Far below, framed by my dangling feet, the muddy waters of the Muskingum shone dully in the weak foggy sunlight of winter afternoon.

Why is it just when a glimmer of newfound hope peeks up at a man, events can sour so quickly his spirits sink back faster than the downward rush of a tall ship's anchor?

A long brown log floated into sight down below, a log with large stubby growths sticking up stem to stern. The wind cleared a hole in the fog hazing the river, and the growths at either end of the log moved at exactly the same instant. Curiosity aroused, I leaned further out for a better look.

My breath stayed of its own accord.

That wasn't a log down there. It was a dugout canoe, and those large stubby growths were not the remains of broken limbs.

They were redskins!

There were five in all. A paddler sat fore and aft. Three of the bloody devils occupied the middle of the vessel. All were clothed in leggins and vests made of bear and sundry other pelts with the hair turned in. The middle three bore arms, smoothbore trade muskets. A rainbow of colors, ranging from vermilion to high yellow, decorated their faces and heads under roached topknots, unmistakenably the paint of war.

The center warrior dwarfed the others. A wide span of shoulders and deep chest stretched tight the skin frock covering his upper body. A necklace of large white claws fronted the brown throat. Beneath a full head of braided hair, his face stood out clearly, painted all in black hue.

The black face had before been a bad omen for white men. The Ottawa, a fierce clan, painted themselves thus as a token that they killed all and took no prisoners. The absence of the black face on his companions meant they would take prisoners if they chose.

A guttural command issued from the Ottawa. The paddlers laid to with hearty strokes and the dugout gained speed and glided off under the fog. None of the members of the war party were aware they had been under observation from above. Thank the Lord.

I laid back and rested my thumping head. While the war party, bound downriver, separated itself from Matthan Hannar with every stroke of their paddle, that was not true of the settlers at Waterford and Fort Frye. An alert had been sounded summoning all able-bodied males to engage in a downriver hunt for Matthan Hannar. Womenfolk and youngsters at Fort Frye would be left under the care of a skeleton militia hopefully strong enough for fending off the approaching Ottawa and his fellow warriors. Outlying cabins inhabited by wives and daughters and youngest sons, if left unguarded, would be in the most danger.

A deep foreboding welled in my chest. I knew full well where the blame for any harm suffered at the hands of the war party by the relatives of those I'd decoyed downriver would come to rest—squarely on my shoulders. No matter what happened, my situation darkened at every turn. Even events in which I played no part threatened to heap further condemnation on me.

Let me tell you, the overly fresh memory of those armed and painted redskins, 'specially that big black-faced Ottawa, put yet one more dose of spunk into tired legs and bones. If those red devils were headed downriver to raid, burn, and loot, they fully intended to escape back the direction they had come. It surely behooved Matthan Hannar to forge on for the cave with the spring—another two or three miles—before engaging any notion of ending the day. I inched back from the cliff, made a crutch of the long rifle, and got on my feet.

The rendezvous with Abel Stillwagon, set for ten days on the bank of Johnathan Creek above the falls of the Muskingum, required a journey of several miles. In the meantime I needed to hang shy of any unnecessary entanglements and circumstances. I couldn't help the Fort Frye settlers in any way. They must fend for themselves, just like me.

Within a mile loomed a familiar landmark. Big Rock, even when obscured by lingering ground fog, boggled the mind. The huge shelf of stone extended far out into the river only to thrust upward and end in a blunt crown of stone fifty feet high. It was as if

the heel of a giant hand had shoved a defiant barrier
into the Muskingum. Big Rock narrowed the river
and shouldered the current hard against the east
bank, creating a chute through which the water shot
in a sea of churning brown foam that tossed off a veil
of billowing mist. Red men and white men, far and
wide, when detailing their travels on the Muskingum, always noted when they arrived and departed
from the site of Big Rock.

Arrival at the renowned trail marker had great
import for my travels. Here the way finally eased for
a while. From dawn through the day I had traversed
wild terrain scarcely touched by man or beast.
Ahead now lay a portion of the old Indian pathway
that ran along the Muskingum a number of miles,
sticking to the highest range of hills along the
waterway. The warrior path lacked great width
since the redskins, whether afoot or mounted on
horses, always moved single file. But while narrow,
the track stood out clearly, worn a foot deep in the
soft places by the passage of moccasined feet and
unshod hoofs over scads of years. I trudged the
pathway trampled by the very redskins I feared,
munching chunks of johnnycake on the march.

As the afternoon wound down, the breeze freshened and quickened and low slate-gray clouds sailed
in from the northwest. A deepening chill tweaked
the nostrils. A norther was brewing just as I'd
speculated last night. The unseasonal thaw of yesterday would be blunted by the norther, a true
blunderbuss of winter capable of burying everything

in inches of snow in a few short hours, rendering movement day or night a trial for even the most seasoned traveler.

A final landmark set my course. Across the river loomed the blackened skeleton of the Big Bottom blockhouse. The redskins had plundered and burned the structure a year ago, January of 17 and 91, when they swept across the ice and wiped out the settlement, slaughtering ten men, a mother and her two children, taking five male prisoners, and panicking the local populace into a sudden retreat behind the hastily built walls of Fort Frye. The fear that black day might be repeated still upset the nightly sleep of young and old clean down to Marietta.

Past Big Bottom blockhouse the path along the top of Wallace Ridge had been marked by the axe of a white man. Each tree on one side of the trail had been deeply notched, pointing the way straight for the cave with the spring. I followed the line of blazed trunks with the very last bit of strength left in me, overcome with weariness, dragging one foot at a time ever forward.

At the sighting of the cave, hesitation and caution skipped off with the wind. I trudged the last few yards to the opening amidst a jumble of large boulders and heaped stone and went in on hand and knee, caring little if any other creature lurked in the darkness.

Matthan Hannar had made his den.

Feeble light bled into the cave through a natural smoke hole in the roof and reflected from spring-

water collected in a large stone bowl jutting from the
rear wall. In a near corner was a faggot of kindling
and a pile of stacked wood left by some passer-
through. Before any other indulgence I knelt on one
knee at the water bowl and drank my fill, waited,
and drank again.

With thirst sated, I set about getting an evening
meal. An old trick of Jeremiah's quickly started a
cooking fire. I cocked the long rifle, plugged the
touchhole, then placed a wad of tow sprinkled with
powder in the bottom of the pan, and pulled the
trigger. Sparks flared down into the pan off the face of
the frizzen and fired the dry cloth. I dropped the
burning coal of tow on the earthen floor and gingerly
heaped cave kindling and oak shavings from the
haversack on the flames. In no time I had an iron
noggin of water for sassafras tea boiling merrily and
bacon crackling in a small frying pan.

The hot tea spread warmth mouth to toe. I chewed
the bacon long and hard, sopped up the grease with
wedges of johnnycake, and gobbled that down too.
After the ordeal of last night and the long march of
today a meal fit for a prince had nothing more to
offer. I licked each finger twice.

The cave was a first-rate overnight camp. Clear
water trickled in through a crack near the ceiling,
trickled down the wall and filled the stone bowl.
Overflow from the bowl, in turn, trickled downward
and disappeared into a narrow channel where the
wall met the floor, leaving the rest of the cave high
and dry.

With a goodly supply of fresh firewood close at hand, I stretched out on the buffalo hide, hair side up, and slept with the lock mechanism of the long rifle, firing pan reprimed, clasped securely between my thighs to keep the powder dry.

Because of all that was to happen over the next few days, it seemed odd later that before sleep hooded my eyes, the last thought in my head was of the Shaw family, father Zebulon, sons Zed and Zeb, and loony daughter Zelda, breakfasting as a family before that roaring fire way back there this morning at the start of my long trek upriver.

Thank the Lord, I slept the sleep of the dead that night with no bad dreams, the blessed gift of total exhaustion.

Chapter 9

Trouble of a different stripe loomed next morning.

I stepped from the cave having slept well past dawn, pleasantly surprised that the ground was still bare. A draft of bitter cold wind nipped at my face. When I looked up at the sky, a bell of alarm clanged in the back of my head.

A low curtain of silvery clouds streaked with darkest gray churned overhead, hurled toward the east by a powerful wind on high. On the ground gusts swirled in one direction, then another. The air was rank with moisture, almost wet when touching bare skin. The norther, arriving later than expected, was about to bust loose with all the fury of hell incarnate.

The coming storm gave me pause. Any hunter caught in the jaws of this approaching blunderbuss without shelter need clearly fear for his life. Now was not the time for rash action.

My mind swept over the terrain ahead upriver, sorting out recollections of journeys by Uncle Jeremiah and Stepfather. The nearest camp offering protection against the wind, cold, and snow about to break over the land lay miles away, a march of four or five hours in the best of conditions. Close was what it would be, a real race to see if I could reach that safe haven before the norther trapped me out in the open to freeze to death.

Was I better off sitting out the storm right here in the cave?

Dare I linger a day and sacrifice the lead I'd gained over pursuit from Fort Frye?

Where were the painted redskins I'd spotted just yesterday? How would they face the rapidly changing morning?

The presence of the Ottawa war party in the scheme of things couldn't be ignored. The savages traveled by dugout canoe and covered considerable distance in short spurts out on the Muskingum. If the redskins finished raiding downriver last night and knew of the cave behind me, they might well abandon the waterway and wait out the storm here in safety, having little cause to fear the settlers would follow them till the storm blew over. The war party was a much greater threat than the brewing norther. I turned back into the cave, somewhat put out about how other people and happenings always determined the fate of Matthan Hannar.

Within minutes I finished a cold breakfast and was on the trail. Since the redskins might next occupy the cave, I left the woodpile depleted and stuffed the remaining kindling in the stone water bowl. I prayed no white settler sought refuge there before the weather cleared.

At the northernmost point of Wallace Ridge, the Muskingum swept by in a wide curve below the high ground. Winds steadily gaining in strength whipped the surface of the river into choppy waves. I leaned against the sheltering bole of a large tree and eyed the brown expanse of water in both directions with Jeremiah's spyglass.

Nothing. No sign of anyone on water or land. For the moment, anyway, the country was mine alone.

"You can't always make tracks when you'd like—by sun or moon. With trouble about, lay 'em when you can, fast as you can, and long as you can . . . and pray your Maker favors you this go-round."

Sound teaching from Jeremiah. And I heeded it. I mean I sincerely heeded it. My pace was quick and stride long.

Though the high ground past Wallace Ridge swung away from the Muskingum awhile, the hill-tops with the ever-present Indian pathway presented fewer obstacles and delays than the bottoms. I stuck up high, tight as a wood tick in a hound's ear.

The norther broke within the hour. Flurries of grainy snowflakes began bouncing about on the gusting winds, and by the time ridge line and river ran back together, the dancing flakes had been replaced by hard crystals of snow that stung hands and face.

Eyesight range dwindled rapidly. Where the face

of the ridge hung out over the rushing water below, I halted, and with one hand shielding my eyes, glassed the Muskingum again. Again nothing in sight in either direction on the waterway. Fair enough. Snowstorms can mask the whereabouts of both friend and foe alike. Speedy upriver travel with little risk of detection was in the offing now.

The sky darkened into a solid gray dome of heavily burdened clouds. Snow came down harder, hissing when it struck the barrel of the long rifle. I stepped up the pace yet another notch. Footing would be doubly treacherous once the ground covered over.

The wind blew without letup. Each gust had a cold hard edge that knifed through the smallest opening in search of skin and bone. I wound a woolen muffler round my neck, donned a fur cap under flat-brimmed hat, and pulled mittens over hands, all without missing a step.

Snow began driving out of the northwest. The leaden clouds lowered till they seemed just overhead, and the sky simply disappeared as slanting flakes exploded into upturned eyes like handfuls of gravel. A layer of white that crunched underfoot buried the pathway. My pace slowed and my stride shortened as the slick snow deepened with each mile.

Short of my destination, much to my dismay, conditions worsened. The raging blizzard, a cornered wild beast growling ever louder, bit and clawed with all its might. Only a thong tied under my chin held my hat in place. Glazed snow rattled off the buttons of my greatcoat. The pathway turned slipperier than sheet ice. My worst dread came true: I was caught in a swirling white cauldron of snow, cold, wind, and ice that promised a stiff and frozen demise unless I got under cover soon, mighty soon.

Not to grind the same axe too often, but I set my feet and harkened back to Jeremiah's tales before the supper fire. How had he described the camp I sought? Had he not related something about its location that would enable me to find it even in the middle of a blizzard? Uncle was always particular, downright fussy, when describing hunting ground and campsite. And why not? He might find himself right back in the same place some storming winter afternoon desperately in need of shelter, just as I was.

I drew his words from memory. "You knows when you're gettin' close. A deep ravine splits the high ground bankin' the river. You gots to climb down the near side of the cut and swing left. Back a fair piece, as the ravine closes up for a quick endin', on your right be a big dark hole. Look close, for an old deadfall slants down across part of the openin'. That hole be deep enough to keep the wind offen you. And fire smoke sifts up through that old tree frontin' the hidey spot 'thout smarten your eyes all night long. No water there. But a fair resting place, nonetheless."

The ravine. The deep ravine. That deep cut in the hills was the key. It was salvation. It would point the way to a safe camp. And once down between the

ravine's high walls I would be out of the unmerciful
wind. Cold I could withstand. But not wind and cold
and blinding snow. Together they made for a hellish
brew, one impossible to swallow for long.

The wind now blew flat with the ground, and icy
snowflakes slashed at cheekbones like tiny arrows.
Eyesight range shrank to arm's length. I moved
ahead, eyes slitted with one hand guarding them,
glad I hunted something at my feet with my head
down.

The raging wind fought me every step but worked
in my favor. I first sensed, then saw a wide black
shadow under the streaming snow. The dark void of
the ravine appeared bottomless, but appearances
didn't matter, down there was a safe haven from the
ungodly weather.

I knotted tying thongs together, fashioned a sling
for the long-rifle and positioned the gun on my back,
then on hands and knees crawled along the rim of
the ravine with my head stuck out over the edge till,
between eddies of blowing snow, I saw a patch of
straggly brush and windswept boulders, possible
handholds for a downward climb.

I sucked in a deep breath, swung legs over the
rocky lip, and eased sideways at a downward angle,
gaining toeholds and handholds more by feel than
sight. A mean and slippery affair, made extra risky
and dangerous by ice-rimmed moccasins, wet mittens, and heavy pack.

Down out of the wind eyesight range lengthened
in spite of the snow and I could pick my course with

greater care. But the brush and boulders aiding my descent petered out and the ravine melded into a long slide of gravel and stone that extended left and right far as one could look. I held still a few minutes, pondering how I should proceed. The slide looked loose, much too loose for my weight. Finally, with no other choice, I eased atop the rubble on my belly.

A slight rumble sounded under me. Without further warning the ground came alive and everything let go at once. Before I could sink in with hand and foot and hold fast, I was trapped in a landslide.

The sliding mass of gravel and stone picked up speed. Sharp rocks gouged my shins, lanced my chin, and peeled skin from my nose. Down . . . and down . . . and down I rushed, belly whopping helplessly along. Just before my teeth rattled loose, everything—gravel, stone, tree limbs, and me—came to a shocking halt at the bottom of the ravine. The jarring stop stunned me from moccasins to hat brim. I rose from the rubble with a string of loud curses and got groggily on my feet. I spat gravel for a week.

After recovering my missing hatchet and making sure no other gear was lost, I sallied forth, feeling downright fortunate. True, my chin dripped blood, my skinned nose hurt something awful, and the places rubbed raw on my shins smarted. But thanks to the heavy greatcoat, there were no other serious cuts or injuries. And I was too shaken up to worry about my pride, which had been wounded considerably.

"Hang with me, Uncle Jeremiah," I muttered. "I'll do better on my own before something stupid kills me off . . . I promise."

Following Uncle's directions I swung left away from the river. The wind howled across the top of the ravine, and the snow, free of its clutches, fell in a thick curtain. I zigzagged through a white tunnel with no roof.

The old deadfall hung upside down just as Jeremiah said, covering the "cavey" hole in the wall of the ravine. This time I didn't charge right in. I poked the gloom back of the snow-covered branches with my rifle barrel, not up to facing a pesky skunk, Lord forbid a bear or painter. Unable to raise a grunt of surprise from anything with fur and fang, I stooped low under the limbs and edged inside.

An upraised blackened fire ring surrounded by rocks the size of piggins fronted the deep hole. Some past visitor had caved in the rear wall and smoothed flat a wide sleeping bench that swept forward within a foot of the cooking ring. A few lengths of dry wood spotted the bench. A snug dry haven, free of wind and snow, good for outlasting a blizzard. Bless you, all who'd come before Matthan Hannar.

I dumped my gear on the bench and laid to. Darkness was at hand and a cache of wood needed gathering. Little was close by in the ravine, and without hesitation I thinned the overhanging limbs with my hatchet, then mixed dead leaves and oak shavings from my pack and fired them, as last night, with a flaming wad of tow.

I melted snow for tea in the iron noggin, fried bacon and ate the evening meal, vowing to snare a rabbit tomorrow for a change in fare.

As can happen after we fight through an episode where danger and excitement push a man at a fever pitch for hours on end, I sunk mighty low staring into the fire sipping the last of the tea, soured and tainted by loneliness. A bitter dose, the loss of Uncle Jeremiah. Linger on his death and I teared up. Uncle had been a true confidant, a well of love and understanding, tough and wise when need be. He'd taken Father's place in my heart. I would forever miss him.

I missed Stepfather too, but he'd come late to our cabin and we'd never become close like Uncle and me. In plain truth Stepfather brought disaster down on all of us by favoring Abel Stillwagon with a seat at the family table. I doubted I'd ever forgive him that.

Sadder yet for me were the leavings of his partnership with Stillwagon—side with Abel or die.

The snow slackened and the wind buffeting the lip of the ravine overhead died away. I slept in snatches, chilled even inside the buffalo robe whenever the fire ebbed, heaping branches on sputtering flames each time I shivered awake.

In the realm of midnight came fitful dreams, a crazy hodgepodge of the sneering Lansford Van Hove, the black-faced Ottawa with the claw necklace, and the hard leathern face of Abel Stillwagon, bald head scarred by knife and powder burns, beard wooly and close-cropped, silver finger ring piercing the end of his long red nose.

Abel's wide full mouth at first creased in a smile of warm welcome. Deeper in the night his flinty eyes peered down the barrel of a rifle held firm against his cheek, muzzle aimed square at yours truly.

Could a savior turn in such a flash? Was this the just desserts awaitin' upriver? Had Jeremiah totally misjudged Stillwagon's true nature?

These doubting questions made for a fretful, restless night haunted by a desperate man's worst nightmare: fear of what morning will bring.

Chapter 10

Near daybreak I was awake more than asleep, a slave of the fire. Faint light peeked through gaps in the deadfall's remaining branches. Some foot stomping and hand clapping got me ready for a meager breakfast of hot tea and cold johnnycake.

The norther left in its wake harsh cold and knee-deep snow that would linger for days. In such extreme weather I had to choose a travel route and future camps with great care. At the same time wild game sought deeper cover and was more difficult to take with trap or gun, so I had to hoard my meager food supply. Even the travel plans of the Ottawa war party would be affected by deep cold and drifting snow. The Muskingum's open waters were for certain their best means of withdrawal, and their retreat would grow more rapid as the river froze and the channel narrowed. Thus, despite last night's dreams and doubts, the rendezvous with Abel Stillwagon was still my best hope for survival. An iffy meeting with Abel paled beside a confrontation with five armed redskins. The faster I joined with Abel and his stiff-legged sidekick, the sooner the odds improved to three against five, a situation more to my liking.

The challenge of the next few days loomed mean but straightforward: outdistance the Ottawa war party, staying out of sight and leaving as little sign as possible; deal with the weather, avoiding calamities such as frostbite, bodily injuries, and starvation; then make the rendezvous site and wait for Stillwagon to appear—and accept or shoot me. A mighty tall order, saying the very least.

Tea finished and gear packed, I checked the priming of the long-rifle and kicked dirt on the fire, reluctant to part with its cozy heat.

Ascending the ravine's northern rampart proved child's play for fresh legs in stormless weather. From the high ground in early morning light flattened by thin clouds, the Muskingum was a broad expanse of pewter banded by mounds of purest white. A touch of breeze wafted from the west as the sun found a hole in the clouds. I glassed the waterway in both directions from an upthrust of boulders, staying below the skyline behind me. Nothing in sight, same as yesterday.

The rendezvous site agreed upon by Stepfather and Stillwagon was a hollow sycamore on Johnathan Creek, thirty miles on eagle wings, a greater distance afoot, and much too far for a single day's hike in present conditions.

Months before, eavesdropping from the sleeping loft, I'd overheard Stepfather and Abel planning their daring trade venture with the Ohio Indians. While Abel and his second partner completed the exchange with the redskins—gunpowder and corn squeezings for hides and pelts—Stepfather was to return home and make certain Hezekial Parsons prepared for a quick sail south on his keelboat with the cargo being carted downriver on packhorses. If he was sure no suspicions had been aroused and the way was clear, Stepfather would fetch such word back to Stillwagon. On the homeward leg and return trip Stepfather had orders to cut and store firewood at selected camps to ease the downward passage of men, horses, and hides.

Their foresight could well prove the best stroke of luck I'd ever been dealt. I carefully recounted each and every word Abel and Stepfather had said that night. If Stepfather obeyed orders (and he was known as an exacting man), the nearest camp he'd stocked from where I stood was ten plus miles away: Rasher Morgan's lean-to shelter. The lean-to nestled off the Muskingum in a shallow hollow, screened by good tree growth beside a stream that never ran dry. Hunting men overnighted in the hollow, knowing they could spring to the defense on short notice—or so Abel Stillwagon claimed.

I closed and pocketed the spyglass, got hat and gloves firmly seated, toted the long rifle across the chest like a redcoat, and taken off for the Morgan lean-to.

Uncle Jeremiah taught that, "When the leaves are offen the trees, no hunter need ever be caught with

his breeches down, ever!" A bright clear winter
forenoon testified to his wisdom. Gone were the
eye-catching, eye-blocking colors and overgrowth of
warmer months. Blacks, browns, and grays held
sway against a solid background of white snow. One
could see astonishing distances into the woods.
Hills, ravines, bluffs, streambeds, indeed, every
break and change in the land jumped out in perfect
detail amongst the bare trees. The trail behind was
as easy to watch as the trail ahead, no small advantage for a fleeing man.

Travel woes underfoot spun another tale. A sheath
of slippery ice underpinned the thick layer of heavy
snow. Every stride required considerable toil and
considerable caution. Dead vines and rock crevices
lay hidden and snagged the unwary foot. Sudden low
spots jarred the whole body. Every trek up slope and
down risked a rump-first sled ride on the seat of the
nether parts. A mile gained seemed forever in time.

I nooned hunkered down without a fire in a
west-facing rock cavity, glad for the touch of warmth
tendered by the bright winter sun. A few chunks of
johnnycake and a slice of pork bacon, washed down
with handfuls of snow, served for the midday meal.
The respite was short-lived; no point tarrying with
the day's journey half completed.

Once back slogging through the snow I stayed on
the trail all afternoon, pausing to search the Muskingum with Jeremiah's spyglass every mile or so,
pushing the pace as much as I dared. I worried little
about leaving tracks there on the high ground along

the river. Water-bound hunters coming ashore shied away from steep gameless places and sought easier passage into the hinterlands by way of the river valley's lower reaches. Tomorrow required a different tack when I approached those inviting lower reaches further north.

The sun kissed the horizon and winter dusk began casting shadows. I wanted to reach Morgan's camp while some daylight remained and confirm Stepfather'd stored enough cordage for a long overnight. Lord, how I prayed he'd followed orders, I was about worn to the nub.

Within the mile three flat hills stood against the dwindling western light one after the other like stair steps, stacking upward left to right. Those hills sat behind the hollow where Rasher Morgan's lean-to nestled. I turned toward them and eased off the ridge line. Daylight's last glimmer faded to black and a gibbous moon rose while I slow-footed downhill.

On the flatland, Abel's "stream that never ran dry," an icy trough in the bitter cold, gleamed brightly in the moonlight and led straight to my destination.

Neither man nor beast presented themselves upon my arrival, and no mark made by foot or paw blemished the moonlit snow. My heart fairly pounded when I found woodpiles on both sides of the lean-to. How Stepfather gathered such a supply of wood without his bloody, hacking cough killing him

was forever a mystery. I recited a prayer of thanks-
giving and laid the supper fire.

Rasher Morgan deserved a plentitude of thanks
too. He'd scalloped out a low mound on the creek's
bank, embedded thick side and rear pickets, and
roofed the lean-to with thin poles fastened with
crosstrees. The open wall faced eastward toward the
creek, the solid back wall repelled west winds. A pile
of stone heaped knee-high curved across the front
opening, hiding light from the fire pit and reflecting
heat back under the slanted roof.

Bless old Rasher. He'd labored building his station
for cold weather trapping till the Shawnees lifted his
hair last autumn. Luckily, the war party left his
shelter intact, probably for their own future stays.
But I was here alone tonight—so far—savoring
every lick of warmth from a roaring fire.

I ate sparingly. A flitch and a half of bacon remained, a panful of johnnycake, and enough sassafras tea for three days, four if watered down. Unless
I enjoyed good fortune hunting or Stillwagon rendezvoused ahead of schedule with a passel of vittles,
Matthan Hannar's backbone was likely to shake
hands with his belly hole before everything was said
and done.

Nothing—not fear of future starvation, not the
risk roving Injuns might spot the fire, not the chance
varmints might scent my food stock and come prowl-
ing about—kept me from a sound sleep. With
enough wood salted away for three nights and a
steady blaze holding back the cold, I snuggled with

the long rifle and sawed the log with the best of them, too warm and content for old nightmares, unaware the bottom fell out of the weather gauge all night.

A loose pole thrashing on the roof and whistling moans at the lean-to's corners jolted me awake right at first light. A nasty rush of air slammed down from due north under a cloudless sky, the kind of fearsome January wind that lasted for hours in dazzling sunshine and locked the land in a deadly killing freeze. I ate a hot meal over flames tortured by raw gusts, then sat back and partook of an extra noggin of tea, readying for a miserable hike into the teeth of those icy blasts: north was my line of travel.

I'd planned a sashay north by west away from the sharp eyes and ears of the Ottawa raiders plying the waters of the Muskingum. But gale winds negated that since they piled snow waist-deep in valleys and bottoms till the flatlands became nearly impassable. Not wishing to buck those drifts all day and night, I donned every piece of clothing possible, tied hat under chin, and marched back for the high ground flanking the river where the wind at least scoured the path clean now and then.

Halfway toward noon, struggling with poor footing, the raving cold, and savage wind, a bad oversight placed me at great risk. In the haste of escaping the lowland snowdrifts I forgot the perils of the Narrows and unwittingly marched into the most dangerous stretch of the Muskingum.

In the Narrows the river ran plumb between tall

hills crowding the banks so close together the shrinking Muskingum appeared to flow under my very feet. From down on the waterway looking up, the slightest movement in the high narrow channel against the skyline and snow-crusted ridges seemed to take place smack in front of one's nose. No place for stealth ever, the Narrows, and passage through there put me at a decided disadvantage. If the water-bound Injuns, who gained miles on a foot traveler in a single day, showed and spotted me, they'd fan out, work a surround, and have my hair pronto. Just as troublesome, I'd reached a point of no return. With pursuit coming from behind (if it was), I'd best forge on past the Narrows, then veer westward and make a lowland sashay after all.

Naturally, once I understood my peril, I snuck a quick downward glance at the river every step or two. And good I did, for I eyed the lumpy brown smudge far back downstream right off, soon as it crept into sight. The legs flapping on that buglike lump were paddles beyond the shadow of a doubt.

A notch in the crest of the ridge beckoned. I slithered into the opening and scrunched down, hidden by a low hummock of broken rock, safe for the moment. Sunlight streamed over the ridge crest above and behind my position, leaving the notch in dark gloom. I trained the spyglass on my pursuers.

What an eyeful. Two paddlers, no passengers. They drew closer. Fur caps, no roached topknots. Closer still. Bearded faces, no war paint, no party . . . the Shaw brothers, Zed and Zeb, in a hurry upstream, rifle barrels protruding from the bottom of the canoe ready for action, heads turning left and right ceaselessly quartering both river-banks.

I was puzzled. I'd expected the war party, not any white men, let alone the Shaw brothers. Why were the Shaws braving the awesome cold and inviting an encounter with hard-knot redskins to chase down Matthan Hannar? A bounty? Gold coin for my head on a platter?

Now something was amiss here. The Shaw brothers might be ornerier than ten-peckered billy goats and always ready for a rough-and-tumble brawl, yet some brains lurked in their upper parts. They enjoyed hunting and eating and funning others enough they'd not throw all that away for what a few gold coins bought. Something other than Matthan Hannar brought them deeper into the Narrows every second. But what?

They certainly weren't on a winter hunt. What then had so roused Zed and Zeb they'd abandoned their own good sense and come charging into territory where they knew the Injuns held the upper hand?

I pondered while they paddled, whiling time away.

If the Shaw boys weren't after me, Zed and his brother clearly sought to overtake the Ottawa war party. But why? Surely not on a lark . . . or a bet . . . or at anybody else's bidding. None of these notions explained a thing. Everybody knew the Shaws wore their feelings on their sleeves, loyal first and always to family and little else, and if they were here in front of me racing after the retreating war party, they did so for personal reasons, some slight, some cruel affront foisted on the Shaw clan by the Injun raiders.

I cut a big sigh, dead certain I'd hit on the answer. Some relative near and dear had been wounded . . . or slain. Maybe old Zebulon himself, even, Lord forbid, sister Zelda. Truth was, nothing short of a family outrage could swing Zed and Zeb this far out of kilter, flying full bore into terrible danger, outnumbered and unconcerned for their own safety.

I couldn't help speculating about what might have happened. Suppose the Shaws—father and sons—answered the summons of the signal cannon and joined the chase after Hezekial's keelboat. Left at the Wolf Creek cabin by herself, what chance had Zelda against five painted redskins hell-bent on murder and pillage?

"None," I lipped silently, "none atall."

Talk about spirits sinking. There was no ducking around it, regardless of what had befallen the Shaws, I was as guilty as the black-faced Ottawa and his painted henchmen.

I squirmed further back into the notch, taking no chances. The Shaw brothers were awfully upset and didn't have any warm hello for me swelling their hearts waiting to bellow forth. Lower than the heathen Injuns was where I stood with them.

Perhaps because it lifted the guilt a mite, one

other thing popped into my head that might explain the rash haste of Zed and Zeb: the off chance Zelda wasn't dead, the red devils had taken her captive. Given how the brothers watched over their skinny sister who even dressed like them, they'd attack an entire Shawnee village in hopes of taking her home safe.

It was gladdening to think Zelda might still be alive. On second thought, that didn't seem likely. The Ottawa's black face argued against prisoners of any kind, and the Ohio Injuns, while known for taking males alive in some instances, seldom had any leanings for sparing females who slowed their withdrawal after the raiding ended.

I shook my head clear. Forget the Shaws and their troubles. Whether Zelda had perished or was in redskin hands, there wasn't one whit I could do to extract a measure of revenge for her or help her enraged brothers retake her. I'd a handful watching after my own hide, and, as yet, hadn't fared particularly well with that simple chore. Anyways, better a live dog than a dead lion (or so Jeremiah said).

Zed and Zeb glided past, paddling hard as ever. I stayed put. Once they were out of sight, then and only then could I show myself.

What next?

The sun stood in early afternoon, the cold undaunting. I had to get clear of the Narrows, off the high ground, and decide on a camp. Trailing after the Shaw boys was out of the question. With the brothers and the Injun war party maybe cluttering the lower reaches upstream, things might become touchy in an eyewink. Backtracking went against the grain. It led me out of the Narrows, but wasted much precious daylight. And just suppose the Shaws were misguided, suppose they'd somehow overshot the Injun raiders in their hurry to find and engage them. The Ottawa and his painted companions could be forthcoming behind Zed and Zeb, hot on their track, planning a bloody surprise of their own when the brothers finally camped and slept.

The best course for Matthan Hannar didn't demand much figuring. Leave the river as quickly as legs could carry me and, never halting, march all night till I made the rendezvous tree, a site far enough away for risking a warming fire.

One last sweep of the Muskingum up and down with the spyglass. No Shaw brothers one way; no Ottawa war party the other. Time to move. I stomped blood into cold-stiffened joints, climbed the rear wall of the notch, and went over the crest behind it, slipping beyond the skyline.

A few miles westward the high ridge line ended. What lay ahead in the lower hills was hellish in the beholding. The wind still slammed from the north, less forceful, but billowing waves of icy frozen snow whipped through the bottoms before it, a force to be reckoned with. I sawed an end off a haversack flap with my knife, cut eye slits, and held the snow mask in place with a tying thong. Then I headed down to buck the drifts.

With the passing of daylight the wind backed

down a notch, then another. The gibbous moon shone high and bright. I plowed north by west, reading the stars whenever the ground swelled enough so my head stuck above the swirling, wind-driven snow.

I disremember the last hours of that twenty-odd mile journey. My legs faltered and breath came in ragged bouts. Hunger cramps had me near tears. Somewhere I lost a mitten. Numerous times I stumbled and fell. A blind, dumb beast was steadier afoot. I pinned my mind throughout on the rendez-vous tree. There shelter from the wailing wind awaited; there bones could be warmed through; there life-staying vittles could be heated and chewed and swallowed; there Stepfather had piled another stock of wood in the hollow of that gigantic trunk.

I found Johnathan Creek the easy way. I tumbled down the bank and came to rest on the ice covering the water. I knew where I was all right, Johnathan Creek was the largest stream emptying into the Muskingum south of the Licking, the wide bed and tree-lined borders unmistakable in the moonlight and swirling snow.

I turned left upstream and walked the black ice. My flagging spirits soared when sheer rock walls rose on both sides and sealed off the moonlight. Those rock walls had a message for me: the rendez-vous tree was within hailing distance.

I spied the dark entryway hole on the leeward side of the mammoth sycamore from the creek bed. I plunged up the bank, trudged the final few steps,

and nipped inside even as I shed my pack, heedless
of any nocturnal guests who had already taken
lodging.

Matthan Hannar lived to fight another day after
all.

Chapter 11

Snow moon . . . cold moon . . . January 17 and 92 was the worst in memory.

The stabbing, pounding, everlasting gale wind regained its earlier savagery and blew for five days and nights without end. Tree limbs popped with the crispness of pistol shots. Dead trees and those weakened by past storms went down in thunderous crashings. Before the big blow ended, first the owl, then the wolf turned mute.

I huddled inside the hollow sycamore over a small fire in a ground hole, buffalo robe wrapped tighter than second skin, burning just enough wood to stay alive, parceling out food in driblets to give innards steady easing, fearful my very shelter might snap like dry tinder. By the morning of the sixth day, the bacon long gone, only johnnycake crumbs littered the bottom of the haversack pouch, too tiny for even a wetted finger. Stepfather's wood wasted away, nothing left but scattered twigs.

The gale finally lifted its smothering hand, and I ventured forth for food and wood.

It was hunt or die time.

The sun ruled a cloudless sky. Frozen layers of snow mantled tree limbs and rock surfaces. Crazy quilt drifts piled high against the banks of Johnathan Creek and ran this way and that amongst the tall trunks. I donned the snow mask against the eye-watering, blinding whiteness shining from everywhere, primed the long-rifle with fresh powder, slung a string of traps over my shoulder, and headed down the rippled ice between the creek's drifted banks.

Woods creatures never changed habits. When deep cold threatened, small game sought the thickets, canebrakes, and cattail clusters in the lower reaches of streambeds. There they took advantage of the thick cover and patches of thinner ice toenails could scratch through for drinking water. Traps set in their favorite winter haunts nabbed small varmints searching for food during night hours.

A long disappointing morning ensued. No wings stirred the air. The wind had rubbed out every trace of game. Cover of any promise along the creek was too scanty for trap-setting. I stubbornly refused to retreat with nothing gained.

By noon I neared the point where Johnathan Creek bustled into the Muskingum. That gave me pause, but unfortunately not for long. I was near starved, hungry enough to risk discovery by the Shaws, the heathen redskins, or any other Jack fool I might meet up with over on the river. So over I went.

The first sign the rest of the day wasn't going to

get much better was the backside of an armed Injun. That spooky sight confronted me partway round a sharp bend in the creek. The fur-covered red devil stood with legs spread, musket leaning against hip, and chewed on a meaty bone of some sort while answering the call of nature. His water splashed on the ice, sizzled, and spawned a whisp of steam between moccasined feet.

Twenty yards behind him, standing straight as a ramrod, rifle uncocked, comforted by the knowledge my approach had gone unnoticed, stood me, one scared white fugitive.

I didn't hesitate. Never taking eyes from him, a long backward step placed the creek bend between us again. As I drew back, the Injun yanked at the front of his breechclout, shouldered the musket, and moved off, gnawing at the blackened bone in his fist. I envied him that meal.

After a goodly spell I peeked round and, no surprise, he was gone downstream, following the frozen creek bed, bound for the Muskingum.

A wise soul would've headed home for the rendezvous tree, gathered branches, stoked up a warming fire, and slept with his hunger till Stillwagon showed in a day or two. But that Injun had meat and somewhere to travel. Where was he headed? Who waited for his return? How much meat did their trail larder hold?

Curiosity got the best of me. It likened the day I'd jabbed a hive with a stick, wondering how bees handled an attack. Not unexpectedly the bees re-

turned the favor and young Matthan Hannar ran for
the cabin a-swarm with white men's flies (as the
Injuns called them). Now, even knowing I'd probably
get stung again, I couldn't resist the urge to trail
after that red devil and learn what he was about.

I'd enough sense not to follow him directly. I
angled cross-country, keeping Johnathan Creek on
the left. A far knoll topped by ragged young trees
overlooked the Muskingum south of the river's juncture with the creek. I crawled the last few yards into
the trees, rifle cocked, spyglass at the ready.

The frozen Muskingum was a wide slab of jumbled
gray ice. Ragged snowdrifts tortured by past winds
wound along the banks. I pocketed the snow mask,
searched where the creek entered the river, and the
red devil I sought centered in my glass. He crossed
the ice surefootedly, eyes fixed on the far bank.

The view over there gave me a start.

A handsome fire burned brightly. Around the
blaze, all busy stuffing their gullets, knelt the black-
faced Ottawa war leader and two others. One eater
sported a roached topknot and slash-painted forehead. The other wore a flat-crowned hat and chewed
with head down, face covered to my glass. Probably
a stolen hat, the bastard.

The topknotted warrior pointed upriver without
rising from his knees. The Ottawa jumped to his feet
and peered the way his companion directed, and I
followed with the spyglass.

The fifth and final member of the war party,
fronting the woods well beyond the fire, signaled

with broad sweeps of a musket held over his head. The Ottawa leader took command instantly. With hand gestures, never raising a shout, he stopped the Injun out on the river, dispatched him up the ice, then grabbed his own weapon and loped to join the warrior waiting at the woods. The two redskins left at the fire resumed their meal.

The Ottawa and his subordinate met and exchanged wriggling hand signs. At a beckoning gesture from the black-faced leader, the river warrior left the ice and joined them. All three melted into the trees like smoke.

Altogether, a most puzzling development. Given the bright winter sunshine, at this time of day— near noon—no four-legged animal it would take three armed men to kill would be out and about. Three of the war party then sought a two-legged quarry, a dangerous enemy, armed as they were.

Lord, maybe the Shaw brothers. . . . Certainly, the Shaws. Who else could it be?

But something didn't seem right. Why face any foe with less than a full force of arms? Why leave two warriors behind out in the open? . . . A trap? Bait to lure in the unsuspecting and spring an ambush?

I swung the spyglass back to the fire. The two warriors left behind hadn't missed a bite. I spotted no firearms about them. They would certainly be tempting for the Shaws, who carried both rifles and belt pistols. The brothers smelled blood at the kick of a bucket. If they were still hell-bent on vengeance, they'd rush into an ambush sure as the sun set in the west.

I hung in the trees, feeling safe watching from afar, held spellbound by what would happen next. Dare I help the Shaws?

A gunshot upstream rent the silence. A nerve-jangling screech from a red-skinned throat followed. Three more muzzle blasts in rapid succession echoed through the hills. The briefest pause. A barking concussion, sounding like a pistol shot. Another Injun war whoop. A second pistol shot. A running fight was under way, moving away from my position upriver, as best I could tell.

Jerking movements at the fire. I trained my glass. The eaters were on their feet, jawboning at each other in loud tones. A knife appeared in the hand of the bareheaded warrior. He threatened his comrade in the flat-crowned hat across the flames. Hat-Injun crouched and stepped back with bare hands shielding his face.

Two distant shots. I ignored them, fascinated by the squabble in front of me.

The knife-wielding warrior began circling the fire, handle held low, blade pointing up. No tomfoolery here. Hat-Injun circled in the opposite direction, still showing no weapon, crouching lower to protect vital parts.

With a long quick stride, Knife-bearer closed ground and swept the wicked blade upward. Hat-Injun tripped and flopped on his back. Knife-bearer leapt atop of him, grabbed for the throat, and plunged his weapon for the gut.

A knee caught him in the crotch and Knife-bearer's head snapped back. A darting hand caught his wrist and turned the knife aside. His weaponless opponent scrambled from beneath him, losing that damnable hat in an escape from certain death.

My hand shook and the spyglass wavered. The exposed head on Hat-Injun was a real jolt. No plucked skull and roached topknot. No war paint. A full growth of short yellow-brown hair framed what was assuredly a sun-bronzed but white face.

Who was this?

The stalking by Knife-bearer began anew, and the yellow-brown head spun around before I got a full-face look-see. One thing for certain: this wasn't a fight to the death twixt two Injuns. Knife-bearer had been left behind to guard a captive, not lure the Shaw's into an ambush.

Knife-bearer advanced, dragging one foot as if badly hurt by the blow to the crotch. Without warning the dragging foot planted hard and true and his free hand snaked out and grabbed the front of his prey's buckskin frock. Knife-bearer tightened his grip, hunched down, and slowly pulled his enemy toward the waiting knife.

Hat-Injun ducked his head, lunged backward mightily, and popped out of the frock like a jack-in-the-box. Bare white skin flashed in the sunlight.

I steadied the glass, holding my breath. They might not be oversized, but those bobbing, sharp-

nippled breasts beating a hasty retreat belonged to
no man. God Almighty, a woman. I raised the glass a
mite. Jumping blue blazes, Zelda Shaw, in all her
unadorned spit-tempered beauty, staring straight
into my lens.

I might have hesitated helping her brothers. I
might not have helped them. But if I was ever to
sleep peacefully again, I couldn't ignore her predicament with the old excuse better a live dog than a
dead lion. Not on your sweet life.

New shooting upstream. I paid it no heed, nor the
danger ahead. I bolted from the trees, hurtled the
snowbank, and landed on the frozen Muskingum,
beelining for that desperate standoff on the far
shore.

The jumbled river ice smoothed out briefly. I raced
onward. Cracking sounds under my feet, spreading.
I ran faster. Would the ice hold? Could I get there
before he killed her?

Knife-bearer grew impatient. He sprang over the
fire, swept his blade in a searching arc . . . and
missed. Zelda glided sideways, putting the blazing
fire between them once more. She leaned and
snatched a burning branch from the flames.

Good girl! Hang on. Hang on, I'm a-coming!

The ice rumbled into hummocks and broken
clumps. Grunting with strain, I picked a path
through the clutter. The snowdrift along the far
bank mounded belt-high. I jumped, landed on my
flank, rolled and came up running. Was I too late?

On either side of the fire Zelda and Knife-bearer

parried and feinted, burning branch against jabbing knife. She held his complete attention.

"Down, girl! Down!" I yelled.

My voice jerked Knife-bearer's eyes from Zelda. He saw me behind her, a wild, crazed new enemy charging in with tomahawk in right hand, long rifle leveled waist-high in left. Baffled and confused by my unforeseen appearance, feeling suddenly under-armed, Knife-bearer retreated, waiting for me to round the fire one way or the other, but I turned his own trick on him, vaulting through flames and smoke, tomahawk poised for the death blow. Caught off guard, Knife-bearer lifted his arms to protect his plucked skull. I slid the long rifle under his up-thrown limbs and pulled the trigger.

The flint in the jaws of the hammer snapped against the metal frizzen. Knife-bearer heard it. I saw it in his eyes. His face clouded as the firing charge ignited with a *fooing* noise. Then the main powder load went off in a deafening discharge.

The rifle ball caught Knife-bearer square in the brisket and rocked him back on his heels. He clutched at the wound, swayed forward, and toppled at my feet in a slack heap, dead before he hit the snow. His long knife skidded off toward a gape-mouth Zelda Shaw.

Zelda sat in a puddle of mud and slushy snow, unaware she was half-naked, dazed by the mind-stopping abruptness with which her death-defying struggle had ended. She seemed near tears. Her eyes looked but saw nothing.

When she started drawing knees under chin, I moved. I'd been through that myself. Once the tears started, a body couldn't hardly not cry themselves out.

I belted my tomahawk, stepped in front of her, and slapped her cheek. Anger sparked in her eyes, but she was back with me.

"Get up and get your shirt on," I ordered.

"Go to hell," she snarled, scrambling to her feet. "Who do you think you be, bossin' me thataway?"

She swelled her chest in defiance, realized her breasts were bare, and spun like a wooden top, frantically seeking her missing frock.

I ignored her and reloaded the long rifle. It was quiet upriver, had been for a considerable spell. Somebody'd won that sharp skirmish, and I'd a hunch the black-faced Ottawa and his friends had mauled her brothers right proper. If I was right, the victors were headed back here at the very moment.

Dressed again in loose buckskin frock with low crowned hat covering yellow-brown hair, Zelda looked a dead ringer for a flat-chested lad of small years. Little wonder she'd fooled the Ottawa war party.

"Who you be?" Zelda demanded, hands on hips.

I hesitated. How would she take learning her savior had caused her captivity? Not well, I suspected.

"Never mind about me. We got to get away from here without delay. The Injuns won't take kindly the killing of one of their raiding party. They'll be back and want our hair, never you doubt."

"Who'd those red devils race off after?" Zelda inquired. I didn't answer that directly either. If she discovered Zed and Zeb had been under attack, Zelda wouldn't budge a puny inch till she knew their fate and how they'd fared. The stiff set of her jaw told that much.

"I don't rightly know, and don't give a hoot about finding out. And neither should you be concerned. It don't matter to neither of us," I lied.

Heat flared in her eyes, her cheeks puffed. I was telling her what to think again and she didn't like it.

Some misgiving beset me. Zelda hadn't made the slightest gesture of thanks for my having rescued her and everything I said garnered a rebellious glare. A testy, unarmed slip of a girl was a burden I'd not reckoned on.

Before she could weigh in on me, I laid hold of her sleeve and shook her back and forth. "Listen close," I commanded, nose in her face, a real trick, slight as she was. "I'm taken out of here. You grab anything that's yours and come along if you want. Otherwise, stay here and before dark they'll bury you and your spitfire mouth with that Injun over yonder." I jabbed a finger at the body of Knife-bearer.

She shook free. "Don't you roughen me. I got no choice but to trail with you, so I will. My brothers will settle up with the likes of you later. I'll get my pot." She tossed me a withering scowl and walked away.

Pot? What was this new nonsense?

Zelda yanked an iron kettle from under a mangy hide. Well, least you cooked in it.

Time was short. I wheeled and headed for the Muskingum. She didn't follow right behind. She lingered at the fire, filling the pot with scraps of meat. She showed more brains than I'd given her credit for.

I waited at the riverbank. She caught up and, without protesting, let me lower her over the snow-bank down onto the ice. I took care she didn't bang me with the loaded kettle. She swung that thing about mighty free. We started through the ice clut-ter, Zelda cursing every step at the weight she toted. I clamped my jaw shut.

A Injun scalp "halloo" sounded behind us, a blood-curdling call like no other, once heard never forgot-ten.

I peered about. Beyond the camp fire at the edge of the woods, the Ottawa emerged from the trees with musket held high in triumph in one hand, and, in the other, what I knew without clearly seeing it had to be a bloody scalp, a Shaw scalp. Beside him, a painted warrior supported a second Injun, obviously side-wounded and hurting. Them Shaw boys hadn't died easy.

When no one answered his "halloo" and he saw Knife-bearer's prone body, the Ottawa shrieked a war whoop and charged forward.

"Run, girl! Run for your life!"

I shoved Zelda in front and whacked her behind

with my rifle barrel. Surprisingly enough, she uttered not a word and set off in a flat-heeled run, covering ground in a hurry, holding the kettle in both arms. I hustled after her. The closest place for a fighting stand with a field of fire was the knoll across the river.

It went well till Zelda's foot slipped and she fell, twisting an ankle. I pulled her up, squatted, and turned my back into her.

"Get on! Hurry, girl!"

She practically jumped aboard. Rightfully scared she was. She hung fast with her legs round my middle and a forearm round my neck, refusing to loose her pot.

Saving the kettle added a heap to my burden. Out on the smooth ice she wrapped her arm ever tighter, shutting off my wind, all the while beating a tattoo on the back of my legs with the kettle.

Cracking sounds beneath us. My scalp prickled. Would the smooth ice hold the weight of two? The cracks spread outward like a star bursting. I took three huge strides and plunged into the snowdrift at the foot of the bank.

Safely on firm footing, I wallowed across the drift in lunges and up the knoll we went. There I pried Zelda's arm free and knelt. "Off, girl! Find cover and hide!" She crawled aside, dragging her pot. Damn woman was determined about that kettle.

I scanned the ice-bound river. They were after us, the black-faced Ottawa, claw necklace bouncing on his chest, and another warrior, the only other mem-

ber of the war party alive and unhurt. They were
still beyond the range of their muskets. But not a
long rifle.

I refused to panic, carefully checking the barrel for
obstructions before repriming my piece. I braced the
weapon against a scaly tree and drew a bead on the
Ottawa. Him I feared most. I wanted no hand-to-
hand battle with that muscled giant.

They rushed onto the smooth ice side by side.
Shooting downhill, I aimed a hair lower than normal
and squeezed the trigger.

Snap—foo—boom!

The recoil lifted the barrel. I ducked under the
haze of powder smoke, searching for my target. The
same instant the ball hit the Ottawa and he
stumbled and dropped his musket, the ice under
both redskins gave way. A huge yawning hole
opened. They sank slowly, the Ottawa unfeeling and
uncaring, his companion flailing madly in hope of
finding a purchase and sparing himself.

I handed the long-rifle to Zelda and swept the ice
hole with my spyglass. A brown arm appeared
briefly, but the hand clawing at the ice stilled and
slowly slipped from sight. Then nothing.

A blow on the head bowled me over.

"You, you bastard!" Zelda screamed, hovering over
me with the kettle drawn back for another strike.

Over the roar filling both ears, I asked, "Have you
gone and lost your tree? You're as loony as everyone
says, aren't you?" I rolled away from her.

That last bit stumped her. "What do you mean,

loony as everyone says? Answer me, damn you," she cried, threatening with the kettle.

"Settle down," I shouted, getting on my knees. "What'd you hit me for?"

"You're Matthan Hannar, that's why," she said. "I knew I'd seen you before. But I didn't know your name."

She dropped the kettle and picked up the long rifle.

"See. Right here on the butt plate, the letters— J.H. J.H. for Jeremiah Hannar, your uncle. I seen you at the fort with him. You be Matthan Hannar, double damn you. Every solitary man in long pants lit a shuck after you an' left me at the mercy of those red devils, you bastard."

Her breath failed her. That, and only that, shut her mouth. She threw down the long rifle and commenced sobbing. Tears wet her bronze cheeks.

I sat watching her, speechless.

Zelda turned away, bawling loud enough they could hear her in Marietta. I settled against a tree. I was tired, she had the old knot on my skull throbbing bad as a toothache, and no one but me was left alive to hear her anyway. So, let her have her cry. She'd earned it; I had to grant her that. I reloaded my rifle and waited for the finish.

Her shoulders finally ceased their shaking. Zelda blew her nose on her sleeve and faced about. She didn't lose a second. "Well, what now? You're damn good at killin' Injuns, I can't fault you for that. But what about me? Do you have any grand plans for seein' me home to my paw? Well, do you?"

I kept my trap shut. Careful, Matthan, careful. Sticking a bare finger in a weasel den was less dangerous than talking with old Zebulon's daughter.

"Well, Matthan. We ain't got the whole blessed day. It'll be dark in a few hours and damn cold to boot."

I saw an opening and jumped in. "Hold your britches, girl. Let a man have an edgewise word." I sucked in some wind.

"We can't get you home by dark for sure and we best make some tracks. Back up Johnathan Creek there's a hollow sycamore big and tight as a cabin inside. Good smoke hole too. We'll overnight in the tree, then see about tomorrow. What you say to that?"

She thought on it, lips pursed. "What about Zed and Zeb?"

"What about them?" I demanded, immediately aware I'd made a mistake sounding angry and anxious.

"They be searchin' for me, that's what 'bout them. My brothers'll never quit lookin' long as they're alive. I can count on 'em," she said, hands back on hips, defiant as ever.

I chose each word with deliberation. "I don't doubt that. But if they find the camp and dead Injun over yonder, they'll read sign and make out what happened. They won't have any trouble telling you went off with someone, or got dragged off. They'll come a-hunting right behind us. Meanwhile we can sleep out of the cold full as ticks on that meat you were smart enough to scavenge. What do you say?"

She took her time answering. "All right. I said I'd trail with you an' I'll keep my word. We can always come back here and meet up with Zed and Zeb." She lifted her brows and cocked her head sideways. "Just one big problem with your sweet plan, Matthan."

I should've known. "What's that?" I reluctantly asked.

"I can't hardly walk. My foot's swoll," she announced.

Before I could respond, she laughed and a sly, cunning smile revealed white teeth. "But since you're two—three times bigger'n me, you'll have to tote me like before, won't you now?"

Lord Almighty, spare me. Once a packhorse, always a packhorse in this woman's feeble mind.

"Get your pot. It'll be dark 'fore we know it."

I at least made her limp over to me. I got her squared away on my backside, iron kettle firmly in her grasp.

"Try not and choke me near to death this go-round, girl," I suggested.

She giggled. "It's Zelda, not girl, Matthan. It not be a hard name atall."

Her heel drummed on my leg. "Giddyap, ol' steed," she yelled, laughing deep in her belly.

I shook my head in disbelief. She was as changeable as Ohio weather. Her mood would switch again. Just wait till she learned about the upcoming rendezvous with Stillwagon. Worse yet, sooner or later, she had to know the truth about Zed and Zeb.

Who said better a live dog than a dead lion? What hogwash. A lion could win the battle, save the fair maiden, and feel sorrier than a dog. Just ask me.

Chapter 12

The march to the rendezvous tree went easily and without undue strain—for Zelda. My part in the long return across the ice of Johnathan Creek proved a hardier outing.

I expected her to chatter endlessly, since she never seemed lost for words and expressed her feelings whenever she saw fit without reservation. But she merely sighed heavily a few times and settled on my back.

The kettle appeared round my shoulder on the end of a skinny, buckskin clad arm. "Matthan," Zelda purred, "carry this for me."

I kept walking, hearing nothing.

She whanged me a lick on the elbow with the kettle. "Matthan, the damn thing be too heavy for me. An' you'll want to gnaw on a bone or two later, won't you now."

I switched the long rifle to my left hand and lay hold of the pot. I was powerful hungry and my elbow smarted right handsomely. The next blow might connect with my crazy bone and raise real havoc. This woman wasn't to be trifled with.

She added insult to injury a quarter mile later. Without so much as a by-your-leave, the muffler unwound from about my neck. She jostled around and a hand slid under my right arm and extended one end of the muffler across my chest. Her free hand met its mate from the opposite side, the cloth band tightened, her hands fluttered, and a large knot appeared miraculously atop my left shoulder.

To my astonishment, Zelda had tied herself securely in place. With another of those heavy sighs, she crossed her ankles in front of me and was soon breathing evenly on the back of my neck, sound asleep. Wherever I was headed, she seemed content to ride along, allowing me to bear the brunt of the work, of course.

I laughed aloud. Matthan Hannar, the great hunter, went out to shoot something for the cooking fire and bagged something he had to carry home, pot and all, and feed besides. What a turnabout.

I followed the icy flat of Johnathan Creek balancing the kettle and long rifle and Zelda, no small feat for legs fast tiring. As I wearied, my sleeping burden provoked more sobering thoughts. While scurrying to save Zelda from Knife-bearer I'd no time to contemplate what would transpire if I succeeded. In one brave swoop I'd shouldered the responsibility for the safety and well-being of a slip of a girl of womanly years with a saucy tongue, who, nevertheless, deserved a better fate than escaping from the hands of the redskins only to face an equally uncertain future with her own kind.

Those who should have rescued her, the brothers, lay dead and scalped, chilling through. And while I'd freed her, I couldn't take her home to Wolf Creek and her father without stretching a rope. What other hope might there be for her? A return trek home alone, unarmed, in this weather? No, that wouldn't do, I couldn't have that. Besides the dangers of the trip, what if she made it to the Shaw cabin and told what had happened on the Muskingum today? Lansford would be beside himself, and when he learned the Ottawa war party had been routed, suppose he and the Ballards and their like found enough backbone to swallow their usual fear of the Injuns and come after me. If they did and met up with Stillwagon or me, the snow would be stained with more blood.

The selfishness wasn't lost on me. My real true concern was my own skin. I'd saved Zelda once, but in spite of my shame at considering myself ahead of a woman in trouble, I wasn't ready to put my life on the line with the Fort Frye mob over her, not yet anyway.

Zelda would have to take her chances on a rendezvous with Stillwagon just like me. If I could keep him from abusing her—or killing her to keep her mouth shut—perhaps I could squire her out of the country, then send her packing for home at the first opportunity. Not an overly promising future for Zelda, no matter how rosy a blush I painted on it.

Lord, what a mess everything in my life had become.

"Matthan, be we near your tree?"

"Not yet. Another mile or so."

Zelda dozed off again and that suited me fine. Maybe she would sleep the evening and night through and postpone till tomorrow any discussion of what lay ahead for both of us. Maybe . . .

We arrived at the rendezvous tree before twilight ran its course. I shook Zelda awake. Without a word she untied the muffler knot, jumped down onto the creek bank, limped across the snow, and disappeared into the entryway hole. Some excited exclamation followed, then she reappeared wrapped in the buffalo robe.

"Damn, warm at last," she declared, swinging her head to and fro. "Matthan, where at is your woodpile?"

I put the kettle down and leaned on the long rifle. "Gone. Ran out this morning 'fore I left on my hunt."

She looked at me in dismay. "You mean to stand there an' say you went off to fill your belly without choppin' the wood first. Be you stupid?"

My ire boiled over. "Now, lookee here . . ." I stammered.

"No, you lookee here," she countered instantly. "I brought the meat you'd have left behind. If'n you want to eat an' not die abed tonight, you better gather plenty, tall man."

Darkness was fast approaching and I was too tired to argue. Anyhow, she was right. In wintertime a wise backwoodser laid in his firewood before the hunt: you weren't likely to starve in one night, but you could surely freeze to death.

"Can you shoot as good as you run over at the mouth?"

"Well enough for standing guard while the gathering be done," Zelda answered.

She held out a hand and I passed over the longrifle. I watched while she pulled the hammer to half cock and checked the priming. Her cunning smile flashed again. "I can always shoot you if the gather ain't enough for two, can't I now?"

Enough of jabbering. I turned downstream.

"Wrong way, tall man," she chided. "What be wrong with the two down trees and old deadfall over there a bit?" She pointed a few rods upstream. "I saw them from atop your back soon as you woke me," she said proudly, eyes sparkling with mischief.

I clamped my jaw, the best way of dealing with her it seemed, and began making the gather for the meal and the night hours.

In short order I snapped two armfuls of branches off the deadfall and fetched them inside. Zelda kept watch and stuffed her loose frock with dead leaves picked from the downed oaks. Tinder, I hoped.

On my third trip she returned the rifle. "Watch for yourself. I'll start a fire an' get the pot stewin'. We'll need two more rounds like that an' at least two hearth logs," she commanded and went inside. What she had to start a fire with, I knew not, but I never doubted she would.

Throughout the cutting of the hearth logs (three

for good measure), I kept the long rifle within arm's reach. Never mind the deepening darkness, I feared the unexpected, which had grown a habit of sneaking up on me the past few days.

Gray puffs wafted from the smoke hole high in the side of the sycamore as I drug the first of the hearth logs through the entryway. A growing blaze heated Zelda's pot seated on a triangle of stones while she sliced deer meat from a leg joint. The source of the knife I never determined, she'd probably tossed the blade in her kettle with the Injun camp meat scraps. Later I discovered she always had with her a small flat tin box containing flint, metal wheel, and cord, the secret means of fire starting she shared with no one. Hard to use, those tinder boxes, took real practice and a steady hand; Mother had learned the trick of it.

The hollow of the tree stretched a dozen feet across and nearly as high. The smoke hole, enlarged by past travelers, was a charred opening near the ceiling opposite the low entryway. Five armloads of branches, the first hearth log, and the cooking fire shrank the room considerably.

Zelda looked around. "Bring in all the logs, Matthan. We'll plug the doorway tonight and make it plumb beastly in here. I be cold since I was took, don't you know."

"Must we sleep standing up?" I pointed and circled my hand, indicating how little bare space remained by the fire.

She smiled, smooth features soft and sweaty beneath the grime. "We can snuggle down together, I won't mind."

"Maybe I would," I put forth, as always unsure of her intentions. I'd been with women of any kind mighty little. She was funning me for certain.

"Hell's bells, tall man," she said, stirring the pot with her knife, face turned away, "calm thyself. I slept ever' night for a week rolled in a smelly lump with them red devils, tighter'n packin' wad, and not a solitary heathen laid hand on me anywheres."

"Perhaps they mistook you for a man-child?"

Her head snapped round. "I'm sure *they* did. But you know that ain't the truth of it, don't you now." She stared me square in the eye.

I felt the red spreading out of my coat collar.

"I'll just have to trust you, Matthan. 'Sides, you don't smell half as bad as them Injuns, though an all over wash might taken the gamey edge offen you somewhat."

I sputtered a meaningless word or two and went after the other hearth logs, overmatched and outwitted. Her tinkling laughter followed me. If I wasn't careful, she'd talk me out of my breeches and put me outside to freeze into stone.

By the time I'd all three logs neatly stacked right inside the entryway, she showed a different demeanor, serious but pleasant. I sat on the logs at her bidding and she reached me a bark slab heaped with venison chunks and steaming bones. I nearly swooned at the hearty smell and ate like a wolf. I licked the slab everywhere when I finished. Zelda chuckled and dipped my iron noggin into the pot. From a leathern pouch she poured a palm full of yellow powder, spilled it into the noggin, and offered the hot vessel to me.

I sipped and grinned in delight. She'd laced the broth with ground meal. "Where'd you latch on to this?" I asked, swirling the noggin before sipping again.

"That's nocake."

"Say again," I said, perplexed.

"Nocake. My mam taught me how. You parch corn in hot ashes, sift the ashes away, and beaten it till fine. Mixed with a little water Zed and Zeb stay right perky on three spoonsful a day. I'd never be goin' anywheres without nocake. Don't you Hannars usen it?"

"Naw," I said between sips, not caring if I burned a lip. "We mostly trail with johnnycake."

"Too much mixin' and kneadin' for maken johnny-cake on the trail," she exclaimed.

She noticed my suddenly stern countenance. "Nothin' wrong with johnnycake atall though, if'n you cooks it up 'fore you taken your leave," she said soothingly. "Your uncle Jeremiah likely was right fond of it."

I nodded in agreement and sipped more broth.

Zelda ate sparingly from the bark slab. "I'd enough for two at the Injun fire an' you ate for two tonight," she explained without inquiry from me.

She wiped her hands on the tail of her buckskin frock, accepted the noggin, and drained the last of the meal-laced broth. "Why you be camped here for so long?"

Full of belly and caught off guard—again—I stalled, searching for the right answer. She'd opened a powder keg that could explode in my lap with one wrong statement. But she wasn't inclined to patience.

"Who you be waitin' here for, Matthan?" she persisted.

"What do you mean?"

"Hell's bells, tall man, you been sleepin' here four—five nights in the middle of Injun territory, you et up your store of vittles, burnt up your wood, an' the storm's blown out. Yet you don't want to watch for Zed and Zeb at the river, nosiree, you fly right away back to this ol' tree like a lead goose . . . why? To wait for someone, I'm a-bettin'."

She dipped a small portion of broth from the kettle.

I had a sinking feeling I was about to step into the proverbial manure pile. Nothing would wait till morning. I might never sleep.

"You're right. I'm here for a rendezvous."

"Who with?" She straightened and balanced the noggin in both hands, interest growing by the second.

My head sank down. No sense believing I could mislead her. No benighted fool sat across the fire. She had a stake in my rendezvous—her life—and she was smart enough to figure as much. Lying wouldn't help my plight, maybe the truth would only

get me stabbed shortly, or later if I ever dozed off. I
returned her intent gaze and swallowed hard.

"Abel Stillwagon," I said in a firm voice.

I waited for the usual flare of temper, the swearing and ranting, the unabashed berating I'd started
to expect every other time I opened my mouth.

None of that was forthcoming. She was suddenly
serious as a funeral minister and shrank down like
a cornered cur dog. "Oh, no, not him, Matthan. Pray
tell, he be the devil's partner. He'll kill me soon as he
lays an eye on me."

"And why would he do that?" I demanded angrily,
puzzled by her total loss of spirit. Something had
gone wrong inside her.

"Because he's never out for good, only evil," Zelda
answered, voice faltering. "Zeb called him 'greasy
pants man,' don't you know." Tears welled.

"Stop that," I snapped. "What's this 'greasy pants
man' nonsense?" My temper began to flare.

Zelda stifled a sob. "Zeb calls him that 'cause Abel
shysters folks smaller and weaker'n himself, an' Zeb
keeps wantin' to wipe his hands on his breeches,
Abel makes him feel so queasy. So Zeb calls him
'greasy pants man.'"

"Abel'd shoot anyone called him that," I blurted,
instantly regretting the whipped-like hunching of
her shoulders.

She steadied herself and dried her eyes with the
back of a hand. "I know, an' that's the black-hearted
devil you wait to rendezvous with, ain't it now." She

paused, shot me a fearful glance, then asked, "What for you want to meet up with him, Matthan?"

I put the best face on it I could. "Abel's my partner. He'll be sashaying by here with his furs and hides on packhorses, and I'm to join him and help work his cache downriver."

"That all there be to it?"

"What else would there be?"

She drew a deep breath. "How come everybody downriver went off to chase you down and hang you? Did Abel have anythin' to do with that?"

I stared, openmouthed. She had neatly led me into a trap and caught me with both feet. How much did she know?

"Who told you any such thing about me?"

"Zeb," she said. "An' Zeb don't lie to his sister. He went off when the cannon boomed then came back for Zed, not wantin' his brother to miss out on anythin'." She cleared her throat and continued. "Zeb told how your step-paw an' Stillwagon took to tradin' with the Injuns, an' General Putnam found you all out. He told how Lansford an' the Ballards killed your step-paw an' your uncle but let you run free. An' my paw—"

I cut in there, having heard enough. "And you've known all this from the beginning and still came off from the river with me."

"Of course, you be innocent."

Dumbfounded by her assertion, I asked what made Zelda believe I was innocent.

"'Cause my paw told me. After Zed and Zeb went

a-barrelin' for the fort 'thout askin' him, Paw said 'fore he followed them Jeremiah Hannar wouldn't abide Abel Stillwagon maken a fugitive outta his favorite nephew. An' my paw don't never lie to me neither."

I leaned back, eased my legs, and studied the top of her yellow-brown head. If she believed me innocent of any wrongdoing, did she harbor any expectation I would forego rendezvousing with Abel and fetch her home instead?

Zelda's patience lagged behind her jawbone. "Don't dare tote me back to Paw, does you, Matthan?"

I shook my head. "They'd never listen to my side of things; Lansford has riled them to a fever pitch and Jeremiah's wounding of the colonel sets all hell to pay in the valley of the Muskingum for Hannars—or should I say for me—the last of the Hannars."

Zelda stared into the flames. "Matthan, I trusts you. You won't abuse me. An' killin' that knife-stabbin' red heathen was a fine piece of work for any borderer. But Abel be as big as two—three men. Can you keep him offen me?"

I took my time answering. She needed some reassurance if we were to sleep atall that night. "Yes, I believe so. Abel must change his plans, he has no choice. He can't make a downriver run with his fur cache any more than I can risk fetching you home. He needs help cross-country with them packhorses."

Zelda nodded, lifted her pot from the stones, and

built up the blaze with new branches. She forced a smile. "Maybe Zed and Zeb will catch up tomorrow and taken me right offen your hands, don't you know."

I looked away and rose, clutching the long rifle. "I'll check our back trail and the woods round about. You make ready to sleep. I'll be gone awhile." Without waiting for any acknowledgment, I stepped outside.

The chance any two-legged enemy lurked about was slim to zero. But the anguish in Zelda's eyes was simply unbearable. She truly feared Stillwagon, and while she trusted my sincerity and earnestness, Zelda doubted one man could handle the giant Stillwagon. I understood that. I wasn't sure any one man could either. In desperation she fell back on the expectation, no matter how weak, that those who'd always before protected her—Zed and Zeb—were alive, searching for their captive sister, and would yet, somehow, arrive to save her. I faded into the night rather than shatter her last prayer for survival with an inadvertent, albeit truthful, slip of the tongue. She'd been through enough for one day. One more soul-wracking revelation and she might turn into a blubbering half-wit, as had many a woman during the Injun troubles.

The clear night was sharply cold, but the air was slightly warmer tonight. Once January freezes bottomed out, days and nights grew warmer a few degrees each turn of the clock till a full thaw melted snow and ice and unlocked the land. Sloughs of mud then formed wherever the sun touched the trail, slowing the travel of men and horses.

By my count the ten days I'd had to reach the rendezvous tree ran dry tomorrow, the eighteenth of January 17 and 92. Allowing as how Abel and his cohort—Hasper something or other—had lost a few days riding out the norther under cover with their animals, Abel would be five or six days late. But Abel had a habit of performing feats other men only dreamed of. Depending on his trail savvy and how bad the storm had blown over beyond the western horizon, he might be only two or three days off.

A speedy arrival of the red-nosed giant boded ill for Zelda, but a prolonged delay before Abel showed, learned his scheme had gone awry, and discovered his tired packhorses must tramp back across the territory to where passage on the Ohio could be secured, boded ill for him and his new and unknown partner, Matthan Hannar. Mud, moccasins, and horse hoofs made for a sour marriage.

I walked far down the ice of Johnathan Creek and dallied till I was pretty certain whatever call of nature womanfolk endured in the night hours had been tended by Zelda, answered my own call, then returned.

A great horned owl hooted. Due east wolves howled, first occasion since the norther. A thaw was just around the corner, sure as midnight.

Zelda had indeed made ready for sleeping. A hearth log jutted into the fire, the branch wood had been rearranged. She lay on the far side of the steady blaze wrapped in the buffalo hide with her head pillowed on one arm. She snored merrily, thank the Lord.

A space on the near side of the fire had been cleared to provide a second bedding site and the hearth log had been cleverly angled toward the open space so it could be slid into the flames piecemeal and sustain the heat overnight. Slid by me, naturally.

The remaining hearth logs, when stacked atop each other, walled off most of the entryway. I removed my greatcoat, spread it for a ground blanket, and laid down with the lock of the long rifle clasped between my thighs.

Zelda smacked her lips, rolled on her side, and the snoring ceased. Her smooth bronze features were startlingly pretty in the firelight. I stared a long while. I'd never known anyone or anything like her. I'd seen a number of women—handsome, fat, ugly, plain, pretty—at Fort Frye, the Point in Marietta, Fort Pitt, and on the Ohio. None had shown any inkling of the spirit and spunk possessed by this slip of a girl—woman. Not a one could've escaped from under Knife-bearer and dodged his attacks long enough to be rescued.

I couldn't help wondering how it might be snuggled down with her as she'd suggested earlier, a notion that shamed me. Enough advantage had already been taken of Zelda to last her a lifetime.

I fell asleep feeling noble as a wharf rat.

Chapter 13

It was anybody's guess which Zelda Shaw awaited when awakening in her company. At the snapping of a twig she could be a calm pleasant woman, a giddy slip of a girl, or a tart-mouthed defiant female. You opened your eyes, grabbed the halter strap with both hands, and hung on for a ride who knows where. She dared the day to be dull every morning.

Like a good lamb I tended the hearth log all night then went hard asleep in the hour before false dawn. A strong hand shook my leg and a high excited voice jolted me awake. "Roust your bones, vittles be 'bout ready." That familiar mischievous giggle erupted.

I positioned myself against the spare hearth logs and faced the fire, surprised at the bright haze of morning light shining through the entryway behind me.

"You overslept," Zelda scolded. "So I fetched the gettin' up eatin' by my lonesome."

My alerted nose scented meat cooking.

"Rabbit stew with a sprinkle of nocake smells

right tasty, don't it now," she declared with another giggle.

"Rabbit stew?"

"Yessiree, tall man. Whilst you snored on forever, I scouted a snow run and snared a lean pair before first light. They be skinny, but they'll chew all right." She proudly pointed to the furry pelts stretched across the branch pile on her side of the snapping blaze.

Her kettle bubbled. She served me on the bark slab and watched me eat. When I returned the empty slab, licked clean, she handed me a steaming noggin.

I sniffed cautiously.

"Black bark tea," she explained. "Mite bitter, but stouter'n melted snow." She was right as usual.

She fed herself, downing a goodly portion, put the slab aside and repeatedly dipped a twig in the kettle and sucked it dry, preferring meat broth to woods tea.

"Matthan," she started, "you said yesterday we'd talk about tomorrow. Well, tomorrow be here, so let us chew the fat awhile."

Zelda's eyes gleamed with anticipation. She seemed downright anxious and I became wary. Something besides a hearty breakfast worked on her. Her voice indicated she had fixed her mind on something and was about to spring it on me, like it or not.

"What kind of fat?" I asked lightheartedly.

Her patience was short-fused as ever. "I got me a

whale of a plan. Your man Stillwagon had to sit out the norther same as us'ens, 'specially with them packhorses he'll be leadin! Likely, he won't show for three—four more days." Words came faster as she talked. "Lookee here, my brothers should be no more than a day behind us at most. If'n we was to make a quick hike back over to the river, we'd likely bump into 'em huntin' for their dear sister 'fore nightfall. Thataway, they'd take me offen your hands and leave you a heap of time to sashay back here to your tree and wait for your partner. An' don't you worry none, I'll raise such a ruckus 'bout them gettin' me straight home to Paw, Zed and Zeb won't be followin' you nowheres, that I promise," Zelda finished breathlessly.

I pondered on a reply, sipping tea, while she wound her hands in the front of her frock. Zelda had planned her proposal with great care and placed her eggs in a single basket: a quick return to her brothers and a fast sweep downriver away from the clutches of the devil's own scoundrel, Abel Stillwagon.

"Well, Matthan, damn it, what you say?"

She'd dropped the fat in the fire. Unless I steered the conversation just so, Zelda would soon learn the true fate of her brothers and I wasn't sure she could face that.

"Too dangerous over on the river. We can't be sure all the Injuns are dead. Best we stay right here and let Zed and Zeb find us." I crossed fingers on both hands.

"But there be only five redskins and we saw all but one dead or badly wounded. How dangerous can one stinkin' heathen be for a man like yourself? Anyways, Zed and Zeb won't have no problem overcomin' that solitary Injun and they'll be near the river somewhere, we just have to help 'em locate me."

I sensed the shape of her thinking. If all attempts to persuade me to spirit her away from the Stillwagon rendezvous failed, she'd head downcreek alone. She'd concocted a rescue scheme suiting her needs, and such was her fear of Abel, she'd sneak off first chance, betting I'd follow and not abandon her to an unknown fate. She didn't believe me capable of the last. Neither did I.

"Girl, what makes you so all-fired cocksure of these brothers of yours? Suppose they've no notion where you are after that storm snowed over all the tracks and closed the river. They might be far behind searching for some clue you're still alive and be days catching up with us. For all they know, the Injuns killed you and the snow has buried you till spring. Maybe they've already closed the book on you and gone home to your paw," I insisted.

"What do you mean, gone home to my paw? Paw'd kill those boys with his bare hands lessen they come home with me kickin' or my dead body. That's the way it be in my family."

My questioning of her brothers' devotion had her blazing hotter than the hinges of hades. Two things were in the fire now: the fat and me. Zelda was a leg up every turn of the wheel. Regardless of how much

I desired to spare her the painful truth about Zed
and Zeb, lest I wanted to play watchdog every
minute of every day and night, she would have to be
told her lifelong protectors were no more. Until she
accepted me as her only hope, no matter how loathsome that was shortly to be to her, Zelda might steal
my coat and rifle in the middle of the night and leave
me high and dry. And if I let her traipse off downcreek alone this far from home without a gun, heavy
coat, and trail larder, I might as soon shoot her
myself.

"Damn it, Matthan, will you taken me to find my
brothers or must a girl do it herself?" Zelda dipped
her twig in the kettle and sucked loudly. "If I be
goin', a late start won't help much, will it now?"

Wondering why the fickle winds of fate found me
in such a predicament, I gritted my teeth and told
her, "No need for you to be so testy. Your brothers
can't help you."

"And why not?" she challenged, voice taut and
shrill.

I laid the truth out. "Zed and Zeb are dead. Slain
and scalped by those same Injuns took you off."

Her head shook back and forth. "Oh, no—"

"Listen to me, Zelda. Who do you suppose those
redskins were battling while Knife-bearer tried his
best to gut you?"

She gave not an inch. "I don't believe you. Even if
it was my brothers, how can you be certain they're
dead?"

"Remember that scalp 'halloo' we heard? Redskins

make that call when they've finished their killing. That big Ottawa was telling Knife-bearer, who was already dead, he'd lifted the hair of white men," I said, hating each and every word.

Tears of dismay and frustration dampened Zelda's face. But I'd spoken the truth and she couldn't deny it. She knew I wasn't capable of mean and deliberate cruelty toward her. Her features saddened and her heart broke before my very eyes, a sight that haunted me for years.

Zelda fell backwards. Before I could move she rolled into a ball, knees drawn tight to breast, and cried in long wailing howls of anguish and grief.

I fled. Nothing in my short life had prepared me for helping others ease the soul-shattering pain of losing those most near and dear. When the heart is ripped from its moorings, first the grief must be cried out. I'd experienced that much firsthand.

I couldn't leave and I couldn't help her at the moment. To keep from some stupid gesture that might only worsen the situation, I gathered wood and suffered with her. The mournful sounds of her grieving trailed after me. I sank lower than a dog's belly that forenoon.

My pile of branches reached shoulder height by the time all noise ceased in the hollow tree. I continued the gather, unsure when Zelda could be approached without inflicting more pain on her.

The first call was almost too faint to hear. The second was much louder. "Matthan, I've need of you."

I eased through the entryway, leaned the long rifle by the opening, and took a seat on the hearth logs, all the while studying her. She had dried and cleaned most of the grime from her face and pounded the dust and wood rot from her buckskins. Her green eyes were clear and very intense.

"Matthan, please listen an' hear me out 'fore I bawl again." Her somber politeness, so out of character, commanded my complete attention and silence.

"I want you to see to my brothers. I won't have them lying dead where wild varmints can worry on them. You be a smart one, you'll find some way to bury them."

I nodded my head, mouth too dry to speak.

"I promise I'll wait here for you. Your man Stillwagon won't be here for a day or two, so I'll be safe enough if'n you hurry back. I'll have the meal ready and waitin'."

Her promise I accepted without reservation. She wanted the remains of her brothers cared for and would behave accordingly. I felt compelled to honor her request as partial amends for foisting a truth on her better left untold. The telling of it had been for my benefit, not hers.

Reaching for the noggin I'd hastily abandoned, I gulped cold bark tea. "All right, I'll be off straightaway. Keep a sharp lookout. If you see or hear anyone, use the buffalo robe for a coat and scoot down the creek until you catch up or meet me coming back." I stood. "An' don't slow yourself down bringing that fool pot with you."

I glimpsed a bleak smile before she nodded agreement, pulled the buffalo robe around shoulders suddenly shaking, and shooed me out the door hole.

A bright sun shone on a warming winter morning. The raw abiding cold of the past week had lessened. Thaws developed slowly but steadily during January in the Ohio country. Creek ice would turn slippery by midday, then freeze solid again at dark.

I set a fast pace and made the Muskingum before noon. From the knoll where we watched the Ottawa and his fellow warrior sink under the ice, I glassed the Injun camp on the far bank. Nothing remained but cold gray ashes around a blackened log. Gone were Knife-bearer's body and the wounded warrior the Ottawa's death companion had assisted back to the fire after the Shaw skirmish.

What happened over there after our departure? Four Injuns I could account for. The Ottawa and two others had ambushed the Shaws, leaving Knife-bearer to guard Zelda. But there had been five warriors in the dugout canoe back downstream days ago. Had the fifth warrior helped with the ambush? If he had, and survived the Shaws' bullets, perhaps he'd returned to the fire, disposed of Knife-bearer, and aided the wounded Injun. Or had another Injun war party made an appearance? I had to learn if new enemies were in the vicinity.

After checking the long rifle, I slid down the

snow-drifted bank onto the frozen river and swung wide of the smooth ice, skirting the yawning hole in which old enemies had perished. No movement in the woods behind the Injun camp. I circled the blackened log centering the ashes, one eye always on the trees.

The tracks told all. The missing warrior had returned. A third pair of footprints extended from the camp, over to the ice hole and *back*, one set deeper than the other, indicating some burden had been given a one-way tote by the final surviving member of the war party. At least three Injuns rested on the river bottom.

I quartered the snow fronting the woods and found the departing trail of the fifth warrior and that of a staggering, half-carried companion. I followed since their footprints led in the direction where the Injuns waylaid Zelda's brothers, my sole reason for being here atall.

A mile or so upstream slabs of rock walled off the pathway. At the base of the wall the Shaw brothers sprawled weaponless, backsides touching. Blood splattered the snow in a wide half circle. Both heads had been scalped. As with everything else in their lives, they'd fought to the last breath and died together. I dragged their stiffened remains hard against the slab wall and covered them with loose stone as best I could. I said a prayer over them, saddened Zed and Zeb had passed on unawares they'd saved their sister with the ultimate sacrifice men made for each other.

When I hefted the long rifle and turned away, my foot struck something hard under the snow packed down by body weight. I knelt, dug under the red-tainted crust, and freed a pistol, wet and ice-encrusted but still in one piece.

The finding of the pistol set my thinking on a new tack. Perhaps the Shaw boys hadn't thrown their lives away for naught after all. A plan for getting Zelda out of danger began shaping in the back of my mind. Giant or not, and trail savvy aside, Stillwagon had surely lost three or four days making our rendezvous because of the norther. That delay gave Zelda a fighting chance.

To reach home alone Zelda needed a weapon, heavy coat, and a haversack of vittles. The belt pistol I'd found and the buffalo hide cut down to size provided the first two. As for the third, I could hunt and rustle trail larder.

Stillwagon probably wouldn't show until the twenty-first or -second. Today being the eighteenth, I'd hunt tomorrow. Early the next morning I'd guide Zelda south a full day, close as I dared draw to the whites seeking Matthan Hannar's scalp, and detail for her the river pathway from our parting to the Shaw cabin. With a gun, coat, and food, Zelda could sit out a new storm or defend herself and be at the Shaw cabin within the week at the latest.

My mood lifted every step along the ice of Johnathan Creek. It had become apparent during my burial mission Zelda and Abel must never meet. From his point of view I offered Abel something useful—a strong back, long rifle, and desperate reasons for siding him. Zelda, on the other hand, posed a real threat. She could tell the truth and hang us all. And Stillwagon had his druthers with women in dire circumstances as he did with lesser men—without hesitation. Whatever else Zelda had endured, including my well-intentioned blunderings this morning, being an Injun captive was not nearly as deadly as being a female prisoner of Abel Stillwagon. He'd see through her "boy" sham instantly.

I was almost high-stepping nearing the rendezvous tree. Smoke puffed from the smoke hole. I circled once about at a distance. No fresh sign anywhere.

Twilight cast an orange glow on the snow. I called out and Zelda answered, her return hello heavy with relief. She'd been aware of my approach, which pleased me.

The scene inside tempered my excitement. The pot that wouldn't be discarded steamed over the fire. But the hearth logs and branch stock had been restacked, leaving a single enlarged spot of bare ground on the far side of the fire. Zelda stood over there, buckskin clothing spot-washed and brushed clean as could be. Fresh bronze skin protruded at her throat and wrist cuffs. She'd scrubbed herself and smelled like fresh mint. A bright ribbon across her forehead peeked from beneath her close-cropped yellow-brown hair. Her cheeks blushed red without pinching or rouge. She flat took my breath away and she knew it. A smile as inviting as virgin snow turned the corners of her full-lipped mouth.

"The meal be ready like I promised." She tamped the ground beside her with a moccasined foot. "Sit here and I'll serve you."

Completely unsettled and sweating like a plow horse, I placed the long rifle and ice-encrusted pistol on the hearth logs and edged around the steaming kettle. What she intended or where she was headed had me baffled, but I heeded her wishes.

She served me and I ate, eyes fixed on her bronze features. I'd anticipated hard and fast questioning about Zed and Zeb, and I wanted to pound my chest and play the hero with my grand plan for whisking her home safe and sound. But she was totally in charge of my every thought and move: I was riding the wagon, not driving the horses.

She handed me a noggin of bark tea, a saintly offering seeing as how my throat was drier than a drought-starved weed patch.

"You found Zed and Zeb?" she asked in a whisper.

"Yes'm," I answered between gulps, amazed at how my heart hammered. I licked my lips.

"Be they gone?" she asked very quietly.

"Yes'm," I croaked, not sure how much to tell her.

"Did they die proud?"

"That they did."

"You saw to them?"

"I covered them with rock best I could and said a prayer over them."

She bowed her head briefly and said, "Thank you. I trusted you'd not fail me."

With that admission the subject of her brothers seemed settled to her satisfaction. Zelda smiled and brushed my cheek with her fingers. "You know, Matthan, your jaw be mighty square and your face a mite long, but the brow ain't too heavy and them eyes plumb bore through a girl."

Never before had she deliberately touched me. She'd hear my heart pounding any second and brand me a fool. I drew back from her hand.

"Sit easy, tall man, I'll not bite you."

Zelda lifted the kettle from the fire, got comfortable with legs crossed, and reached for the noggin and a share of bark tea.

She sipped and swished the tea in her mouth, face creasing with pleasure.

In a calm voice I told Zelda how I'd stepped on the buried pistol, how that untoward incident fostered a plan for her safe return downriver, how that plan would protect her from Abel's wrath and unseemly desires, how I'd help her home sure as sunrise.

Zelda heard me out. When I finished, a single tear spilled from the corner of her eye. She swiped it away and said, "Don't surprise me none. You'd never abuse a girl nor let her be mistreated."

My chest swelled. Her belief in my true feelings about her kind soothed lingering guilt about the harsh treatment I'd doled out earlier.

She placed the empty noggin with the kettle. "Matthan, shuck your greatcoat. We'll need it for a

blanket along with the buffalo hide. You best see to
yourself outside, then barricade the door, don't you
know."

I shed the coat, bolted through the entryway hole,
and gulped a heap of night air. I expected a hail of
laughter to follow right behind, but all was quiet
inside. Soon as my breathing slowed I removed my
frock and scoured face, neck, arms, and shoulders
with snow, dancing with cold.

Before I finished I stopped still as a startled elk. If
I stepped back inside I realized my life would be
forever different no matter what took place between
us. When you started across a shaky bridge, you
made the far bank or took a powerful dunking.
Either way there was no turning back.

An owl whirred overhead, seeking food as he did
every night. It came on me some things were as
inevitable as the owl's nocturnal hunt. I was here
and she was here. Tonight was tonight . . . and
tomorrow was tomorrow.

I slipped the frock over my head and stepped back
inside.

The fire burned low, embers waxing bright then
dull. I positioned the hearth log and barricaded the
doorway with branches to keep varmints at bay.
When I turned, Zelda said, "Come here, Matthan. I
be cold."

That was nigh onto impossible to believe. After all,
she had both the greatcoat and buffalo robe. When I
circled the fire she swept back the robe, reached for
my arm, and tugged me down beside her. Soon as I

was in place, she covered us both over and snuggled against me.

"Hold me tight, Matthan."

I lay hold with both arms, smelling her hair and the scent of mint.

She passed an arm round my neck and said slowly, lips moving against my chest, "Don't think poorly of me, tall man. There be wonders a woman has to know the truth of least once in her life, don't she now."

And the night began.

Chapter 14

January 19

Cold metal jabbed my cheek and awakened my senses. Groggy with sleep, I turned facedown, but the sharp jabbing pressure persisted. I pried an eye open, thoroughly puzzled.

The double click of a pistol cocking replaced puzzlement with outright alarm.

Abel Stillwagon had his unannounced partner dead in his sights, caught abed unarmed, was my first thought.

The pistol was withdrawn and a familiar voice said, "Fret not, tall man, I don't aim to shoot you, just be sure you keep your promises."

Anger cold as the pistol barrel clogged my tongue. I rolled into a sitting position. Zelda sat on the last hearth log, framed by morning light through the door hole, aiming the weapon I'd so obliging provided dead center on my bare chest.

"Overslept again. Won't never learn, will you now."

The pistol had been dried, cleaned, loaded, and

primed, undoubtedly with powder and ball from my horn and shot pouch. The end of the yawning muzzle was just beyond reach. Dangerous, this female. She'd shoot me if I gave her cause, last night or no last night. Never two mornings alike, I reminded myself, never.

I donned my frock, hoping her grip would waver. She held steady as a rock. "All right, what is it you want from me?"

Her face hardened, green eyes deadly serious.

"Let me hear you say it one more time. I won't have you think me a weak-willed hussy not deservin' of proper respect and throw me over."

My mind reeled in wonderment. It was my turn to smile. "I'll help you back to your paw. I'll keep my promises, just like you have."

She uncocked the pistol with both hands. I reached for the weapon, but Zelda pulled back. "No need for a woman to surrender her protection, be there now?"

I nodded agreeably. Long as the hammer wasn't dogged back, she was safe to be around unless riled over something.

Zelda stewed the last of the venison bones and rabbit meat, and brewed bark tea in the noggin while I made a scout round about. The air was cold but slightly warmer than yesterday. The thaw continued. Warmer weather meant better hunting. A kill today would stock Zelda's trail larder and tide me over till Stillwagon arrived.

Throughout breakfast the giddy slip of a girl Zelda returned and chattered about the upcoming trek downriver tomorrow morning. The affair of last night and the episode with the pistol garnered not a single word of recollection. If either had ever taken place, it seemed true only on my part.

I went hunting convinced what could be said with certainty about Zelda depended on the moment: today foremost in her thinking was our departure tomorrow; and she'd proved she could load, cock, aim, and fire that damn pistol if need be. About anything else connected with her I was completely puzzled and uncertain. She baffled me time and again.

After our comings and goings the day before and the lack of game sign downstream on my previous hunt, I headed the opposite direction.

Johnathan Creek wound and twisted back on itself every whipstitch. In several brush clumps and canebrakes along the bank, I set foot snares and overhanging neck loops that could be checked on my return, and again early next morning. Small game preferring night and dawn feeding might be out anytime in the thaw, desperate for food.

A mid-morning hunt in brilliant sunshine through snow crunching underfoot added up to less than ideal conditions in which to seek bigger game. But deer and others not hibernating had to eat too. If whitetails had bunched together anywhere nearby, after being snowed in for nearly a week, browse should be getting scarce in their parks. When it was feed or die, even big animals grew careless.

The creek looped out of sight into narrowing higher ground. I headed uphill and made a stand above the streambed, downwind and screened by brush and tree trunks, rifle across a low oak limb, primed and ready.

An hour passed. Numbness beset my feet. I propped the rifle against the oak tree and stuffed hands in coat pockets. Even in the midst of the thaw, it was raving cold.

Low yapping from northward, upstream. I pushed the snow mask above my ear and leaned to listen. Louder barking . . . wolf sound. Brush crackled and a white-tailed doe landed on the frozen creek ice. She jumped forward on three hooves, right foreleg broken below the knee. Wolves flashed to either flank and lunged, fangs bared.

The larger gray wolf sank his teeth into flesh and ripped downward, toppling the doe. She fell on her side and skidded on the ice. The smaller wolf was at her throat in a hairsbreath. Another powerful ripping of teeth and blood spewed on the ice. The doe jerked and twitched then lay still.

The wolves tore at their kill. I got rifle and tomahawk in hand. Hope you're right, Uncle Jeremiah. Here goes! I let out a mighty yell and went down the hillside straight at them.

Both heads lifted and they stared at me, muzzles dripping red. Seventy feet separated us . . . fifty feet. They growled and snapped their fangs. Thirty feet. More fang snapping and growling. Fifteen feet. Never halting I brandished the tomahawk and screamed aloud. Their will finally failed them and the wolves broke. They scurried upstream right before I decided maybe Jeremiah's contention wolves were always more afraid of men than we were of them was pure poppycock. I knelt gasping for wind and watched the beasts lope out of sight. They'd circle back and watch from cover, that was their way.

I rolled the doe on her back and gutted her, then peeled the hide. Heart, liver, quarters, and choice parts I piled on the hide and tied off with a leather thong. I'd been plain lucky taking prime big game without burning powder.

The sun was past its zenith and camp five to six miles downstream, leaving enough time before good light slipped away to lug the bundle back and start Zelda cooking and smoking meat for tomorrow's trek.

How I wanted to share my luck with her. She had every chance now of getting home. Hunger was the least of her worries. I taken off down the creek ice, already feeling the heat of the cooking fire.

In my excitement to see Zelda again the bundle on my back weighed less than a feather. Patches of slick ice slowed me a little, but as I neared the rendezvous tree I was almost trotting. One long creek bend remained.

A pistol fired, barking report echoing in all directions. Zelda had fired a shot. At what? Fear knotted my innards. She would shoot only as a last resort, knowing full well if she missed whatever threatened would be on her before she could reload. I shed the bundled meat and sped down the slippery ice, cocking my rifle as I ran.

I cleared the creek bend and packhorses blocked the way. Pure panic rippled through me. Great God Almighty, Stillwagon! He'd shown but a day late after all.

Hasper whatever-his-name fronted the horses, facing away from me. He had the lead reins of the pack train in his teeth and swept his upraised rifle back and forth, trying to draw a bead on someone over by the rendezvous tree. I slid sideways to see over there too, and drew down on Hasper with my gun.

The immense bulk of Abel Stillwagon's backside was unmistakable. His legs were thick as tree trunks. Blood stained the buckskin covering the back of his left shoulder. Zelda hadn't missed with her only shot.

Abel skipped sideways, light-footed as a deer, and stepped toward the rendezvous tree. "Gotcha, girlee," he boomed triumphantly and turned slowly toward me and Hasper, dragging a sizable object through the snow with one huge paw.

It was Zelda, of course. The beefy fingers of Abel's right hand were entwined in her close-cropped, yellow-brown hair. He jerked Zelda to her feet without losing his grip. A broad, leering smile curled his lips. The silver ring in the tip of his huge red nose sparkled in the sunlight. "Frolic for tonight, Hasper, my son, frolic for tonight."

"That'll be enough of that," I said with as much bluster as the fear choking me allowed. I kept my rifle on Hasper.

A moment of puzzlement and surprise swept Abel's face. He recovered just as quickly, jerked a long-bladed knife from his waist belt with left hand and pressed the cutting edge to Zelda's throat, trumping my move slick as a whistle. My rifle should have been trained on him, not Hasper, a man showing me his backside with his gun aiming the wrong way.

A quiet spell longer than life itself passed.

Abel sighed. "Once an enemy, always an enemy, young Master Hannar. Turn and shoot him, Hasper. Let us see how much he wants the lassie to live." A deep laugh of triumph bellowed from Abel.

"No, don't—" Zelda gurgled.

Hasper started to turn about . . . I made my decision. I wasn't any good to Zelda or myself dead. I dropped the muzzle of my rifle so I couldn't miss and shot the turning Hasper through the lungs. His gun discharged into the snow as he fell.

"Lookee here, fool," Abel shouted.

I looked. The knife whipped across the bronze skin of Zelda's throat, stunning me to the quick.

Abel held her by the hair with one huge hand at the end of a fully extended arm, utterly scornful of the life he'd just taken. Zelda dangled in midair, the wound in her neck a gaping, jagged, mocking smile of sorts, all her limbs a-sag, lifeless as a wooden doll attached to a string of yarn in the hands of a child. But she couldn't dance anymore like children made other dolls and suddenly I hated Abel more for that than for killing her, and in the next heartbeat I went plain flat crazy with rage.

Caution and fear swallowed by blinding fury, I whooped and charged, rifle reversed and held overhead for the death blow. Abel stood rock still. His flinty eyes never wavered. The knife whipped again as he cut a wide swath across Zelda's forehead at the hairline in a brazen attempt to scalp her. More red welled and coursed down her face. I was a madman with one single narrow glimmer of thought: kill the bastard.

Abel flung Zelda aside, switched the knife to his right hand, and dropped into a fighting crouch. Too crazed for clear thinking, I tightened my grip on the rifle barrel and brought the stock down in a killing arc. Abel blocked the blow with a loglike forearm. The rifle stock shattered and the biggest piece struck his right hand, dislodging the knife.

My forward rush carried me against his chest. It was the same as running square into the side of a barn. With a snorting grunt fit for a devil, Abel wrapped his huge arms round me, locked his hands behind my back, and bore down with all his awe-some strength.

I'd already lost my wind crashing into his chest. My lungs burned. Rising gorge blocked my wind-pipe. My eyes turned back into my head. I swam in a sea of red, going nowhere. This was the end.

Abel's grip eased and his crouch deepened. He drew in a mighty breath and lowered his head to begin the final squeeze to death. His beard scratched down my face.

I was lost, without hope. He started to tighten his grip and sour breath from his nose wet my forehead. In a final halfsecond of desperation, even with arms encircled and legs bent at the knee, I realized it was hurt him badly or die. Too spent for butting with my head, I extended my neck and clamped onto his huge red nose with my teeth.

I put every essence of my being into that desperate bite. I ignored the pain of his crunching embrace and tightened my jaws. My teeth sliced through soft flesh. With the last trace of my wind I strained hard as I could and my teeth met. I ground back and forth once as blackness dulled my senses.

I was falling. Cold ground soared up and smacked my cheek. Somewhere way off I heard howls of pain. They weren't mine. Something was choking me. I couldn't think straight, but I wasn't dead and I wanted to breathe. I tried to spit and couldn't empty my mouth. I reached between my teeth with hooked fingers and pulled out a lump. I forced an eye open.

In my reddened fingers was the entire end of Abel's nose, silver ring still in place.

A roar of pain caught my attention. I raised my head. Abel was on his side, both hands covering his bearded face. Blood streamed between his fingers. A hand shot out and he pulled his knees under him. He was getting to his feet.

I forced myself to move. He was recovering. Soon as he found me alive, rage would give him renewed strength; he'd never quit till he killed me for what I'd done to him.

I cast about for a weapon. My gun lay in pieces, ruined. Hasper had triggered his off as he fell. Leastways I seemed to remember that. Abel's knife I couldn't locate. Maybe it was under him. What then? I needed a killing weapon and needed it now. I felt my belt. Both my knife and tomahawk were gone, lost in the fight. Abel was trying to stand. I rolled onto my knees and felt around, shaking my head clear.

My searching fingers finally bumped something cold and hard and sharp, the blade of my tomahawk. I laid hold of the handle and lurched to my feet.

Abel had fallen back on hands and knees, still overcome by the pain of his severed nose. The effort of standing got my innards jumping. Blackness edged in on me again. I took two shaky steps then another.

He never did know I was there. Without any hesitation I drew back and buried the blade of the tomahawk where his neck met the base of the skull.

Abel died without sound or protest. His arms spread apart and he settled on his face. The tomahawk held fast.

I took a step backwards and the blackness came over me in a wave. I was out cold before I thumped into the snow.

Chapter 15

I was somewhere else for a spell, lost in a black hole. The stomping of hoofs and a horse nickering brought me around. I opened my eyes on a site ripe with violent death.

Hasper lay on his back, sightless eyes wide open, reins of the lead horse pinned beneath his body. The pack animals had grown restless with thirst and hunger.

Abel sprawled facedown, a bulky heap capped by the protruding handle of the tomahawk. A wide band of blood had dried on the side of his neck.

Zelda rested on her side in front of the rendezvous tree, her whole front smeared with red. Her once pretty face was a horrible sight even from a distance.

My innards heaved and emptied themselves. I turned my head and threw up into the snow. I rolled away from my own mess and chewed snow to cleanse my mouth.

I sat with arms clasping knees till my innards settled. Abel had bruised me everywhere above the waist, yet no bones grated and my spittle was clear

of blood. Every move would hurt for days, but I'd
live, no matter how sad and meaningless that appeared there in the last hour of daylight.

The cold deepened as daylight dimmed. A wolf
howled upstream. The lead horse nickered and raked
a hoof across the rein pinned under Hasper. His
companions stamped and whinnied. Their nerves
were fraying. Unless tended to quickly, they'd break
free and run off in all directions, taking with them
not only the fur cache but also whatever foodstuffs
Abel had with him.

But first, Zelda. I couldn't leave her body, cut to
pieces and uncovered, out in the open another minute.
I'd damn well gotten her killed and because of that it
wasn't in me to insult her memory by tending the
horses before her, no matter how valuable the animals were.

I went over to her, legs wobbly, breathing pain-
fully. Abel hadn't missed putting hurt in a single
muscle or limb of my upper parts.

I knelt on one knee beside Zelda, reluctant to even
touch her. Abel's attempt to scalp her had failed. A
bloody furrow showed where his knife had scraped
across the top of her forehead just short of the
hairline. White bone peeked through the cut. I
gently rolled Zelda onto her back.

The sight of all that blood around her throat and
on her chest set my innards churning and I almost
missed the fluttering of her eyes. I ignored the
movement, counting it as one of the strange things

others had seen dead bodies do. After all, I'd watched Abel slash her throat ear to ear.

I was sliding an arm under her back when her eyelids fluttered again and tried to open. That I couldn't ignore. I yanked my arm free, pulled her frock back with both hands, and lowered an ear to the cold skin of her bloody breast. I held my breath and listened as close as I ever had in my whole life. Nothing. I pressed my ear harder against the cold skin. Deep inside her I heard a faint thumping, weak but steady.

She was alive, barely so, but not gone yet.

I drew back and wiped at the neck wound with the top of her frock. Abel's knife had sliced from under the ear down the side of the neck, struck the breastbone and skidded sideways atop the bone at the base of the throat, thereby missing her windpipe, then coursed upward again through the soft flesh on the opposite side of Zelda's neck. What a relief. The wound was mind-stopping ugly, but not in itself life ending. Most dangerous was the loss of blood from the cuts on her throat and forehead. That might kill her yet.

I swept Zelda into my arms, stepped inside the rendezvous tree, and lowered her to the buffalo robe beside the fire pit, personal hurts forgotten. An armful of branches stoked embers into a hot blaze. I removed my greatcoat and covered her.

Doctoring was mostly a mystery to me, but I'd heard and seen enough to know Zelda needed something to spark her, something to warm and nourish

her inside, to get her fighting for her own life. I
jumped from foot to foot thinking. Corn liquor had
done it for Jeremiah and Stepfather. But I had none.
Or did I? Hadn't that been the raw smell of corn
liquor on Abel's breath nearly gagging me as his
powerful arms squeezed the last bit of wind from
me?

I hurried out to the packhorses. They were still
strung together in the same line, restless as ever. I
sidled over to the lead animal, talking gently to him.
Once I had hold of his rope halter, I patted him on
the flank, untied the bundle on the pack trees
straddling his back, and let it fall to the ground.

Talking all the while, I rummaged through the
bundle. No corn liquor. No furs either. Each pouch
contained a collection of ornaments and trinkets,
necklaces, arm bands, even drinking cups, all made
of silver. A whistle escaped my lips. So Abel had
traded his corn liquor and gunpowder for far more
than just furs and hides—or he'd stolen the silver
treasure from the Injuns. Either way the contents of
the two pouches was worth a small fortune.

I moved to the second packhorse, freed his bundle.
There I found what I sought. One pouch contained
Abel's food larder. Nestled in the second were two
earthen jugs with wooden stoppers. I pried the
stopper of one free and sniffed. Sure enough, corn
liquor of little age, if judged by the nose-wrinkling
smell.

Back inside, a soft flush spread over Zelda's ravaged skin. She was soaking in the heat. I held her

head in one hand and tilted the jug. She swallowed
but a tad, still enough. The balance spilled down her
chin and ran into the open wound on her neck. She
twitched violently, a worry-easing sign for me for
sure.

I pillowed Zelda's head on the rolled edge of the
buffalo robe. A wolf howled, closer by, I believed, and
a horse whinnied. It was near dark and unless I
moved quickly I'd be chasing horses for hours.

A long night lay ahead. I started a fire with a
flaming branch just beyond the rendezvous tree and
piled it high with faggots from the gather I'd made
while Zelda cried over the deaths of Zed and Zeb.

Abel's rifle stood against the far side of the tree,
put there as he cornered Zelda with both hands. The
weapon matched my shattered long rifle. A quick
looking over revealed he'd given his prime gun
painstaking attention. A beaded sheath of leather
covered the lock and three brass moons decorated
the stock.

The horses and recovery of the bundled deer meat
came next. Once I finished dragging the bodies of
Hasper and Abel into the brush across the creek, the
pack animals settled considerably. Among the furs
bundled atop the third horse were hobbles, bells,
picket ropes, and ground pegs. I arranged the horses
in a loose semicircle facing the fire, ground-reined
them on long leads and pegs, then hobbled them. All
of them began digging in the snow for browse,
hopping about in short jumps as hobbled animals do.

I fashioned a torch by wrapping the end of a

branch with a swatch of fur and dousing it with corn liquor. It was full dark and the moon not yet showing when I went after the bundled deer meat. I beat the wolves there by a whisker. Two pairs of yellow eyes glowed in straggly cover just beyond the fading light of my torch. I retreated with rifle ready.

The moon rose and I spent an hour or more cutting cane for horse feed in a brake along that last long creek bend above camp, Abel's rifle within arm's reach at all times. The wolves stayed clear, not bold enough yet to show themselves, and I finished the cutting and divided the cane amongst the ravished pack animals.

Zelda burned with fever. I forced a few more drops of liquor down her. Her breathing was shallow, her heart faint; she was too weak to open her eyes. Now and then she mumbled, the words too garbled to understand. Finally, she slept. If she lasted till daylight, the spitfire had a chance. I knew nothing else to do for her. I didn't bother washing her wounds, sleep seemed more important for her that night.

I roasted deer liver and heart on a stick, downed them, then cooked slices of front quarter and ate my fill. Afterwards, I brought Abel's larder inside for safekeeping, stacked the silver pouches and fur bundles against the rendezvous tree, and heaped more wood on the outside fire.

Worn-out and hurting all over, I dozed beside Zelda till past midnight. Wolf howling roused me. The horses stayed in place, nervous but too tired for venturesome doings. I built up the outside fire again, then slid the hearth log ahead inside.

Sweat shone on Zelda's forehead and cheeks. She awakened, looked at me without recognition and went right back to sleep. The fever had a powerful grip on her. Dawn would tell the story for her.

Before sleeping again I wedged Zelda's pot in hot coals beside the hearth log and boiled chunks of deer meat, preparing broth for the next awakening.

First light found me chopping cane above camp. The early morning air was the warmest yet, and with some hearty blows I chopped a hole through the creek ice nearest the horses. While they chewed cane, I led them one at a time to the ice hole for a long drink.

The horses were a solidly built lot, firmly muscled, free of pack sores and well gentled. Hasper had obviously lavished care on them, probably on strict orders from Abel. Stillwagon was known for better treatment of his horses than his fellowman or white women. Few folks beyond Fort Pitt would miss such a brute. It shamed me the Hannars had ever had any dealings with him for any reason, good or bad. Scheme with the devil and you might burn forever in the nether reaches of hell. As I might yet. The Fort Frye crowd wouldn't heap any praise on me for killing Abel and forget other transgressions like the Injun trading and robbery, not by a long sight. Guilt was guilt to their way of reckoning.

I stepped through the door hole expecting Zelda's fever had lessened. The heat in her had worsened

instead. Sweat poured down her face in rivulets. Her
breathing seemed weaker. One look and I knew she
needed more care. But what? I fought down a surge
of helplessness and determined anything was better
than nothing. When sick animals grew too cold,
Jeremiah warmed then. When they got too hot, he
cooled them.

I grabbed the noggin, fetched cold water from the
ice hole, and splashed her face and neck. The water
washed away the dried blood. The cuts had dried
over and showed no festering or proud flesh, signs
Jeremiah always watched for. If Zelda hung on till
the fever passed, she might survive.

I carried water from the ice hole countless times.
Every now and then she'd commence shivering and
I'd hold her close and rock her. Soon as the burning
took hold again, I plied her with cold water. At
midday and twice well into the next evening and
night she swallowed a few sips of meat broth.
Through it all her eyes never opened.

In between times, I gathered wood like a crazed
squirrel collecting acorns and fed and watered each
horse at least once at the creek. I slept in snatches of
a few minutes here and there.

Just before dawn the second day, a calm came over
Zelda. Her breathing finally deepened and her cheeks
were cool to the touch. I hated to leave her for any
length of time, but I did long enough for a scout
round about in all directions. We were alone in the
midst of a white-blanketed wilderness beginning to

run wet with melting snow. The sun had a brassy hue at daybreak.

The outside fire burned down to coals. I fetched wood for the cooking fire and Zelda's eyes were not only open, they followed my every move.

She appeared terribly small beneath the folds of the greatcoat. Her features were white and drawn, green eyes hollow and rimmed with black.

"I must look a sight," Zelda murmured.

"That you do," I agreed. "But you're alive nonetheless." I dipped the noggin in the kettle and slipped down beside her. She managed three goodly swallows with me holding her upright. I wiped her chin and got her settled again.

Zelda opened her mouth, but I shushed her, refilled the noggin, and talked while I chewed and sipped. "Stillwagon and Hasper-whatever are dead and gone. How doesn't matter, they're stiff as logs. That leaves me and you and four good pack animals. You're mighty sick and will be weak for a long while. Best we get you home and a roof over your head. A thaw has set in and the weather will change. Trust me, it'll come up a rain sure as sunrise and every creek twixt here and your cabin will be waist-deep with runoff in no time atall. We taken out of here early tomorrow and we can reach your place in three days before the worst of the wet weather hits."

Her eyes widened and she shook her head side to side.

Before she spoke, I started right in again. "I'll cut that hide robe down so you'll have a coat and tie you on a horse. We've got to move, girl. I can't be sure the Injuns aren't following Abel with a mind to steal back those hides he traded for. And your paw can tend you regular," I added.

Of the silver cache I made no mention. The riches in those pouches outside complicated things a mite. A sick and weakened Zelda had to be taken to the very doorstep of the Shaw cabin, increasing the danger someone would see me, and, if being spotted downriver was dangerous before, it was doubly so now. Suppose my shirttail cousin Hezekial Parsons had knowledge of Abel's scheme to gain possession of the Injun silver. If Hezekial caught wind I was back with packhorses and no Stillwagon, he'd hire the Ballards and send them after me. Maybe he couldn't deal with me out in the open and risk sharing a hanging rope, but Hezekial would try to steal the silver with others of his own ilk. His gold was as good as Colonel Van Hove's where the Ballards were concerned. I wagged my head in dismay. I was still fleeing for my life, but now in the opposite direction with the Injuns behind and white men up ahead. Nobody'd believe my story on a deathbed.

Before she could protest my speechifying, Zelda drifted off to sleep. Her breathing was steady, her color good but not flushed, and her forehead was clear of sweat. She looked as peaceful as an angel.

I spent the morning gathering firewood, chopping a new hearth log, and cutting cane in a brake further upcreek. My snares held two rabbits, which I cleaned, skinned, and cut apart for stew. Along with the

jerked meat and Injun pemmican in Abel's larder,
we'd enough food stock for a week on the trail.

In the bottom of Abel's larder pouch I discovered a
muslin sack filled with ground meal. I switched the
meal to a leather bag and washed the muslin cloth in
the ice hole. Zelda would want to cover that ugly cut
clean across her forehead soon as she made ready to
leave the rendezvous tree. The collar of the buffalo
robe was high enough to hide her neck wound. She
set store by her appearance on occasion, and I
wanted no delays when it was time for weighing
anchor. She might still surprise the daylights out of
me, but I was beginning to understand her somewhat. Just somewhat, not a lot. She certainly handled
a lot easier flat sick on her back. Hard to be cantankerous with your eyes closed, don't you know.

Zelda slept the day through. I made a late afternoon scout, saw nothing of interest, and after feeding the pack animals, boiled a kettle of rabbit and
deer stew seasoned with two handfuls of Abel's meal
and salt from one of Jeremiah's little glass jars I'd
had in my haversack since leaving our cabin way
back when.

At dusk Zelda's eyes popped open and she ate like
a starved woods rat, chewing fast and furious. She
finished, wiped her mouth with the back of her
hand, and smiled wide. "Lordy, that was tasty."

I passed her the washed muslin cloth I'd dried
over the fire before she awakened. Her eyes fairly
shone at the sight of it. "For to cover your head
wound," I stammered.

"I know, I know," she exclaimed. In no time she had the cloth tied in place. Her appearance was much more pleasant with that nasty knife slash covered over.

But even that little bit of excitement took its toll. She was suddenly tired and flopped back on the buffalo robe. "Lordy, I be all in and I've hardly moved a lick."

"I'll carry you out to your horse in the morning," I reassured her. "With your legs tied under him, you can ride up there like a king in his carriage and chew on dried meat and pemmican all the while. It'll be the easiest chore you've faced in many a moon."

"It won't be anything such, but if that's how you see it, fine with me. I won't be left behind, don't you know," she said.

"Girl, if I never finish anything else in all my born days, you'll live to see the smile on your paw's face when we ride up in front of your cabin. Your brothers and Abel and Hasper and a passel of Injuns lay dead across half the country hereabouts, but you're alive and kicking, somewhat feeble I admit, but still drawing breath, and I aim to be sure one good thing comes from all the killin's been done, no matter who had a hand in it. Do we understand each other?"

Either she was too tired to argue or didn't figure she could win this time around. She nodded and said, "We'll do it your way, tall man. It's what I asked of you all along. Let me sleep till I'm hungry, won't you now?"

With that, she smacked her lips, buried a cheek in the hair of the buffalo robe, and dozed off.

I heaved a big sigh and drank my way through a warm noggin of bark tea. I'd climbed back into that box with no lid: I'd made a promise I'd keep even if it cost me my life. Something about this slip of a girl-woman got deeper and deeper under a man's skin the longer you were around her. She drew you to her like the heat of a fire on a cold night. There was no turning away without thinking a heap less of yourself.

And with that realization I rekindled the night fire and fed the horses, stirred by my deep feelings for her, but at the same time awed by the fearful burden being responsible for another, particularly a woman down and hurting, placed on a man. She was the biggest challenge of my young life.

Chapter 16

January 24

Zelda called for food short of midnight. She did herself proud, then squirmed deeper into the buffalo robe. I felt her cheek with the back of my hand and found it cool to the touch. My hand lingered and she gave me a soft warm-eyed smile before turning and falling asleep.

All her rest was necessary. Once under way tomorrow, the nearest camp with good shelter was Rasher Morgan's lean-to. Between here and there awaited a sight of open country.

A thin crescent moon hung high and the melting snow glistened like crystal in the silver light. The air was warmer tonight than last as the thaw deepened. A few spotty clouds scuttled across the face of the narrow moon. Rain was a few days away, but coming nonetheless.

During the night hours a new problem arose. The outside fire held those creatures who prowled the darkness at bay, well away from the hobbled horses. But across the creek where I'd dumped the bodies of Abel and Hasper I heard movement and low growl-

ing. The thought of wolves and other varmints
worrying their flesh sat poorly with me. Those were
white men just like me, lying exposed for all comers
to push the brush aside and gnaw on. Something
had to be done for them.

I set about a search of the fur bundles stacked by
the rendezvous tree. Hidden deep in the last bundle
I located what I was sure Abel had stashed somewhere in his cache—a small keg of powder. Old
war-horses like Stillwagon never lacked a powder
supply when embarking on a long downriver journey. The keg of powder solved my problem come
daylight.

In the coldest part of the night just before dawn, I
was hard at it preparing for a departure shortly
after first light. Each horse had to be unhobbled,
watered at the creek, led back, and tied in line. I
positioned the wooden-treed pack saddles on each
back and secured them with cross-strapping and
belly cinches. Lumping the fur bundles in a single
load freed a horse for Zelda. The silver pouches,
hobbles, and sundry equipment made a second saddle
full. The final riderless animal carried our food
larder and the corn liquor. I left the pack animals
lined out, munching the last of the cane, and went
inside for Zelda.

She sat upright beside the dying fire, buffalo robe
about her shoulders, boiled rabbit meat in one hand
and iron noggin in the other. "I'm ready," she said
quickly round a mouthful.

"Good, we've got a twenty-mile ride ahead. Stand so I can make a coat for you."

With her hands full, the robe fell at her feet when she stood. I stepped behind her, held the robe full-length, and marked where she needed armholes with the point of my knife. A few fast slashes here and there and the robe was a coat complete with slots for a rope waist belt.

She finished the rabbit, dropped the noggin in the kettle, and slipped both arms through while I held her new coat. Zelda knotted the rope belt and exclaimed, "It be heavy, but it feels good, tall man."

I pointed through the door hole and followed her. She waddled in the heavy robe-coat, but she'd not suffer from cold during daylight. The muslin cloth was a white band circling her head.

I boosted her aboard the lead horse. Zelda took note of the soft pelt I'd tied over the wooden center-pieces of the pack saddle as she swung her leg across the animal. Dressed in buckskin breeches, she rode astraddle like a man without any concern for appearance.

Zelda raised an eyebrow and without a spoken word between us I retrieved her kettle from the rendezvous tree and tied it atop the food larder packed on the horse directly behind her. "I'll probably be buried with the damn thing," I muttered.

She heard me and laughed heartily for the first time in days. She was as ready for a long ride as I could get her.

I stepped to the head of her horse and fisted the

lead rein, Abel's long-rifle cradled in the crook of my off arm. I looked back at her. She knew by my expression my mood was suddenly serious. "I've a chore needs doing before we're off. But first I'm gonna put you out of harm's way."

I worked the pack train, tied head-to-tail, down the ice past the creek bend closest to camp and tied Zelda's horse to a tree trunk slanting out over the frozen water. The ice was thawing, but would hold horse weight another day at least.

I handed Zelda the long rifle and backtracked upstream. Dragging Abel and Hasper free of the brush and back across the creek set me to sweating. I shed the greatcoat, pulled and tugged their stiffened bodies through the door hole, then placed them beside each other. After covering them with every last speck of remaining firewood, I fetched Abel's powder keg, freed the stopper, and trailed a line of black powder twixt the entryway and their resting place. Next I wedged the keg between them, taking pains to ensure the powder trail ran right under the open hole in the upended keg.

A thin branch burst into flame soon as I stuck it in the glowing embers of the cooking fire. At the doorway I stopped and lighted the powder trail. It flared and hissed and I grabbed my greatcoat and ran for Zelda and the horses.

I drew near them, donning the greatcoat on the move. Before Zelda could ask for an explanation of my disappearance a deep, booming explosion shook the ground. A shaft of flame thrust above the trees and brush screening the camp. A column of black smoke billowed upward behind the widening fireball, and the top of the rendezvous tree swayed but didn't topple. The gun-broke pack animals fidgeted a bit and held steady. The crackling of a fast-burning fire reached us.

"Matthan, what in hell's name be you doin'? Any Injun within miles of here can spy that smoke and know where we be," Zelda observed in her old tart-mouthed fashion.

"Never you mind. I couldn't leave even scoundrels like Stillwagon and bent-footed Hasper where the woods beasts could have at them. They was white men same as your brothers."

Hurtful memories dropped her head and she sat quietly while I tied her feet together beneath the belly of the horse. "We must get along right smart and put a heap of territory behind us. I won't halt lessen you yell out. We'll noon when we reach the high ground overlooking the Muskingum short of the Narrows and not before, you understand?"

Zelda nodded and handed me the rifle. In return I pulled her brother's pistol from a pocket of the greatcoat and handed the weapon to her. "It's loaded. Stick it in the front of your coat. If anybody or anything waylays us, wait as long as you can, then shoot and hang on to those crosstrees till I reach your side." She nodded again and followed orders. Her face had a wan look already. She was in for a mighty mean time of it.

There wasn't any grass growing under our feet,

but I whistled up the horses and taken out of there downcreek.

Despite his questionable and brutish character, at horse handling and training, Stillwagon was one of the best. The pack train clipped along steadily without any misbehavior, surefooted and big of heart; they worked at things right proper. Their breath puffed in the damp morning air. Before reaching the juncture of the creek and the Muskingum, we halted just once for load balancing and a tightening of holding straps and belly cinches. The morning sped by.

Zelda rode slack-bodied, head bobbing when she slept briefly, hands locked on the saddle trees. No word of protest or complaint passed her lips: she'd do to ride the river with.

At the Muskingum before we began the climb for high ground, I shook her awake, got a couple of jolts of corn liquor down her gullet, and handed her a rabbit leg. Eyes watering from the liquor, she smiled her thanks, mighty weak but sincere as all get out.

The longest and roughest part of the day's journey awaited. The river ice showed dark patches here and there, sign frozen water was melting and weakening, and stretches of massed and jumbled ice chunks made for much zigzagging travel and wasted time. The high ground, while cut by a gully here and there and scored with piles of rock rubble at certain points, was safer and more favorable for pack train travel. So to high ground we went.

It took some scrambling and hard breathing, but

the horses made it up there. I gave the animals a blow, got them lined out again, tied one of Zelda's wrists to a saddle tree so she wouldn't tip over and hurt herself, then led off down the ridge line. The winding trail had softened in the weak winter sunlight but as yet hadn't turned to slush and mud. That came tomorrow if the thaw persisted.

I held the horses at a right smart pace for the half dozen miles before reaching the overlook above the falls of the Muskingum. Water swept from under gray ice and cascaded over the rocky falls into an open expanse of black water. Below the wide pool another bank-to-bank sheath of solid ice extended onward, unbroken, round a far river bend. Not a living thing moved anywhere in the valley of the river, upstream or down. The silence was almost unnerving.

Zelda was awake, barely, face flushed and shiny with sweat. I untied her wrist and she began rubbing it. Her smile was weak at best. "I watched a man with a pointy beard at Fort Pitt. He drew pretty pictures with charcoal on parchment," she said. "Just like that." She nodded down at the water coursing over the rocky falls.

Such spirit plastered a smile on my face. "How 'bout another slug of Monongahela straight from the jug? You seem a tad worn-out."

I fetched the liquor jug from the following horse and handed it up. She drank a swallow, too large, and coughed furiously. She squeezed her eyes shut and downed a second sip, a smaller portion this time. With a fiery breath, Zelda handed the jug back. "Do put fire in your gizzard, don't it now?" she mouthed in a strained voice. "I was too sleepy last time to know what bit me."

Letting the train have their blow, I retied the jug atop the larder horse and brought Zelda jerked beef and pemmican for chewing on the next leg of travel. She remarked on how good the horses looked after five solid hours of movement.

"They're well rested and been fed good," I told Zelda. "We'll test their mettle before the day is over. We're sticking here on high ground and beelining for the Narrows. We'll noon late, but even then they'll likely not get a drop of water till we reach the Morgan camp. Be a dog-tough traipse, but we need a roof over your head tonight."

I reached up and placed a palm on her forehead. Her color was better and the sweat had dried on her. "My maw always felt me for fever," I explained.

She got that real soft look round the eyes and covered my hand with one of her own. "Why, tall man, I believe you might feel pretty fair toward me, don't you now?"

I pulled my hand free and stepped back. "And I believe you're ready for getting along the trail a piece, woman."

She shook her head in exasperation. "Zelda, Matthan, Zelda. It not be a hard name atall."

I spun about, hiding red cheeks. She giggled as I clucked the lead horse ahead. She was always too quick on the uptake for me. I held the upper hand when she was sick or asleep, hardly auspicious tidings for the future. It was a goodly thing she was leaving off at her home place.

Drainage gullies slashed the high country preceding the Narrows and slowed our pace considerably. Shallow waters from melting snows ran through the gullies and spilled down the ridge faces into the river. Every so often the steepness of the crevices forced us westward till we found suitable crossings. Rugged travel well into the afternoon, a jolting, jerking ride for a woman weakened by past afflictions. Zelda rode light as possible, but the dreaded flush regained her features and she sagged between the pack saddle trees, nose hanging inches from horse's mane.

The last gully before reaching the Narrows ran shallow and wide with water and we made a late nooning there. I freed Zelda's feet and lifted her down. At first her legs failed. She held tight on to my arm and stamped feeling into her feet. I leaned her against a handy tree and saw to the horses.

The animals weren't tucked up yet, and with no time for pack removal and a true rest, I watered them one at a time in the shallow gully where melted snow flowed fresh and clear. After each horse drank his fill, I led them away from the water, then saw to Zelda.

The gentle breeze blowing from the southwest had stiffened and gained a biting edge, the first signal the thaw might not continue. Colder air was in the offing for tonight with wet weather coming sometime soon. Zelda needed a dry camp at the Morgan lean-to more than ever.

She sprawled on her rump against the chestnut trunk. Her head hung between raised knees and a shiver coursed through her. I clasped an arm, pulled her on her feet, and bent over in front of her face. Her eyes drifted shut again. "You're beat. I know that. But you've got to move about and get some meat in your belly. We're not there yet," I warned.

Zelda's head started to droop and I shook her hard enough to rattle teeth. "Wake up! You'll not give out on me, damn you. Being a woman don't cut you any extra with me."

The old Shaw dander flared just as I'd hoped. "Go to hell, tall man. I'm just nappin'. Stop blabbin' and fetch me some grub," she snarled in a single breath and commenced walking in a tight circle.

I stifled a grin and fetched cold meat and a handful of ground meal. She ate and walked at the same time.

"Keep at it. I'll be back shortly."

With rifle and spyglass, I trotted down the winding trail till I reached a spot affording a clear view of the first stretch of the Narrows. I glassed the sun-dappled ice and both banks a section at a time. No movement as far downriver as the next bend where the ice swung eastward out of sight. I trotted back, anxious to complete the day's journey while daylight lasted.

The wind blew harder and the clouds thickened, still white but higher and wider. Zelda was walking her tight circle, arms clutched about herself, but her pace had slowed greatly. She had little fight left and needed hot vittles and a long warm sleep. I doubted she could travel two days in a row.

With that in mind I gave her no slack at the moment, much as I disliked rough ways when a woman was involved. But we had to make the Morgan lean-to with its cover against the rising wind as soon as possible. A good chill might bring back her fever with a vengeance.

"Let's shake a leg. This wind will last into the night. We'll not halt till we reach camp." I avoided the sight of her worn, haggard features and boosted her into the pack saddle. She didn't quarrel when I tied her wrist to a crosstree and her legs under the horse's belly.

"Just remember, up ahead there'll be a fire and hot tea and a dry, tight bed. You can sleep long as you like. All right?" I waited till she bobbed her head, then led the pack train into the Narrows.

Tanking up had freshened the pack animals and put spring back in their hocks. I took full advantage of their renewed vigor and kept them moving as fast as the winding trail allowed. So concerned was I about reaching camp, I fretted not an instant over the chance other white men or the Injuns might be on the hunt anywhere near. I couldn't hardly turn the pack train on the narrow pathway anyhow. Straight ahead was it for now.

Zelda slouched in the saddle the farther we traveled. We cleared the Narrows just before sunset and she called out. When I halted the train she handed down the pistol, which was poking her hard in the middle, and slumped across the horse's neck. The sweat pouring down her face and soaking the head-band, unchecked by the chill whistling wind, frightened me. She was sickening fast. I tied her other arm down and we taken out once more.

I turned the horses when I spied the stair-step hills against the faint light remaining behind the western horizon and wound downhill to the creek fronting Rasher Morgan's lean-to. I barged right in, taking no heed, counting on a deserted camp. Luckily, it was: no sign anybody had been there since my departure days ago.

This go-round I ignored the horses and tended Zelda first. I freed the fur bundles on the last pack animal and toted them inside for bedding, then cut Zelda loose and carried her in. Plenty of the wood cut by Stepfather remained along the sides of the shelter and I had a fire popping in short order. While water boiled for tea, I rubbed Zelda's arms and legs and wiped sweat from her brow. She was too tired to help.

I forced a goodly portion of tea laced with meal down her and settled her under the buffalo robe. She seemed as weak as the day she'd been slashed and nearly scalped and that bothered me greatly. I wanted to fetch her home, not kill her on the trail.

She spoke my name in a hoarse whisper. I leaned an ear close above her lips. "Where be my pistol, tall man?"

I shucked the weapon out of a coat pocket and placed it square on her breast. The corners of her mouth curled in a faint smile. "Thank ye," she mumbled.

I went to see after the horses, feeling somewhat better about things. There was some spark, no matter how feeble, still aflame somewhere deep inside that girl-woman. She amazed me at every turn.

Chapter 17

January 25-27

The night passed without incident. At dawn I made my decision. The weather remained unchanged and likely better than we'd see for days, but without at least a full day and another night of rest I dared not move Zelda. She had eaten almost nothing since our arrival and tossed and turned and sweated for hours before falling into a deep exhausted sleep. Somehow her fever hadn't returned, but I didn't trust it wouldn't.

All morning, like a bad tooth left unpulled, the wind blew at its whim, whipping and gusting, ruffling the long hair on the rumps of the horses. Those poor beasts waited patiently in the lee of the lean-to while I cut and carried cane for them. They'd probably never known the comfort of a barn or shelter of any kind. They withstood much with little complaint.

The nagging, biting wind did shred the smoke from our fire. Nonetheless, past noon, with Zelda sleeping soundly and the fire burning bright, I made a scout over along the Muskingum, looking for trouble before it found me.

I was hiding in a stand of hickory, checking the river bottom for intruders, when brush rattled across the ice-bound waterway. Noise carried astonishing distances in the river valley, even with a brisk wind blowing, and I held fast, listening and glassing the far bank section by section. I wasn't budging till I was certain a four-legged animal made the disturbance.

My ear caught the sound of new movement. I trained the spyglass on a marshy bottom notching the low hills over there and looked and listened a long while. Brush rustled and swayed, and I went right on looking and listening.

A white-tailed buck shot from the overgrown mouth of the marsh and hesitated on the splotchy river ice, as frightened by the slippery footing as whatever pursued him. His hesitation made for a perfect target.

A flintlock fired.

The deer's legs went rigid and he fell sideways.

The brush parted and a greatcoated hunter stepped into sight. I didn't need spy out the sparse black beard, long nose, beady gray eyes, and flesh white as milk. The filthy bandage tied beneath the chin and masking half his face told the story. Who else but Joseph Ballard suffered from a broken jaw not yet healed?

The buck had been hazed from opposite sides and forced from cover. So, if Joseph was on the left,

brother Timothy was on the right. Sure enough,
Timothy pushed aside heavy brush and stepped onto
the frozen river. He leapt back as the ice cracked
beneath him. Joseph roared with laughter. The ever
solemn Timothy spat in embarrassment and walked
toward his brother.

Together they tugged the dead buck from the ice
by the rear legs and gutted him. Timothy stood,
looked inland, and whistled shrilly. In no time atall
two other hunters, one stooped and rail-thin, the
other blocky and long-bearded, joined the waiting
brothers. Working swiftly in the late afternoon light,
the newcomers strung the deer by the feet, head
flopping loosely, on a long pole and trudged eastward
away from the far bank. Joseph and Timothy stood
guard fore and aft while their companions did the
heavy work.

I stayed perfectly still, shaking like a leaf trem-
bling in the wind. If there were four of them, more
waited in camp over yonder. During Injun scares,
white men hunted in large parties and took game
quickly by driving it toward each other. Downed
animals were whisked back to camp for skinning
and smoking then carried home under heavy guard.
Lucky for me, the Ballard party hunted the low hills
and marshy bottoms on the eastern bank, which
placed the melting ice between them and the Injun
path traversing the highlands over here. The Fort
Frye hunters were familiar with Rasher Morgan's
lean-to in the shallow hollow behind my position.
But his death at the hands of a Shawnee war party

just four months ago was fresh in their minds and scared them enough they shied clear of it. They were hunting meat, not a shooting fight with the Injuns.

Taking no chances, I glassed the river and both banks till near dark. Once convinced all the Ballard party had returned to camp for the night, I headed for Rasher's place and Zelda.

The fire burned low and the hobbled pack animals eyed my approach. A furry lump in the center of the lean-to reared upward and a yellow-brown head popped into sight. "I'm hungry," Zelda called.

She'd slept the clock around twice, her only nourishment a few slurps of broth taken in a half stupor. Her eyes were clear and face free of sweat. The natural rosy tint of her cheeks was missing, but she appeared rested and sat upright on her own.

Zelda caught my nervous glance back the way I'd come. "Something the matter?"

I dropped wood on the fire. "We've got company."

Fear widened her eyes.

"Go easy," I said quickly. "They're not Injuns. Hunters from downriver, Fort Frye most likely."

Zelda pulled the buffalo robe chin high. "Did you see any of them? . . . Know their names?"

The quaver in her voice puzzled me. She knew Zed and Zeb were truly dead and gone, and accepted that. The quaver wasn't excitement then, she was scared of something.

"You dislike someone particular from Fort Frye?" I got water boiling in the noggin and sliced venison into my small frying pan; I'd lost a taste for boiled meat the past few days.

"Not many a man can be trusted on the best of days. I've learned to take a mighty long look at things whenever menfolk in numbers come around."

That was all she revealed about some past scare or hurt she'd not forgotten and I didn't push further.

"Well, damn it, tall man, did you recognize any of them?" The close check she kept on her temper slipped a little. "Weren't considerin' lettin' them take me offen your hands, were you now?"

She'd seen inside my head as if there were a big hole above the ear. I was considering that very possibility at the moment. If they could "find" her at a place of my choosing, while they saw her home along with the bounty from their hunt, I could make a run westward and get clear of my fellow men once and for all.

"I'll snitch on you lessen I know who they be, Matthan. And I can tell when you lie."

Her threat made the truth my only choice. My escape plan couldn't work without her keeping a close mouth about my being in this part of the territory.

"Two of them are brothers, Timothy and Joseph Ballard," I confessed.

The gaze I got in return would've scalded rocks. "I'll not stand for them bein' near me. Them two hunt with a sorry lot, all the riffraff without women of their own. My paw warned me 'bout the likes of them."

Zelda squared her shoulders and jutted out that bronze jaw with the finely honed mouth. "Matthan, you promised you'd fetch me home. I'm holdin' you to your word, tall man."

I shouldn't have expected anything less. Whenever she was fully awake and in possession of her wits, she constantly backed me into a corner, lost for words, sullenly angry at her skill for turning any devious intention on my part to her advantage.

I turned the venison with the point of my knife, dillydallying while I scrounged for some clever way to regain the upper hand. "All right, you've kept your word, I'll keep mine." Before she smiled in pure triumph, I said, "But you travel when I say so and listen tight every step of the way. You understand? I'm not longing to learn firsthand how it feels when a rope saws your windpipe in half."

I set the frying pan on a flat rock next to the fire. Her green eyes were somber and heavy all of a sudden. "I'll not bring harm on you and break my own heart, Matthan."

Those words cooled the steam in me. I hefted Abel's rifle. "The horses need me. You eat, then get back to sleep. We're taken out of here before first light."

I ignored her disappointed frown and moved off. The horses were thirsty and starving. And they didn't talk back. Nor did they jolt a man where he lived with a look and a few words.

Dark clouds swept across the first quarter moon. A chill wind, heavy and clammy, never slackened. The weather seemed stuck in the same rut, but I'd a hunch when it changed we'd not like it one bit. Cold days with wet snow lay in wait, the worst weather for travel short of a norther.

The cane I'd cut before the river scout held the animals in good stead. Once fed, watered at the stream, and rehobbled, they settled for the night, sleeping on their feet. Enough cane remained for the morning feeding, which eased my mind. The sound of chopping carried a far piece in these hills, maybe clean across the Muskingum. Now that the Ballard party had settled in across the ice, no sense inviting them over unexpectedly before we were well under way in the early hours tomorrow.

The empty frying pan and noggin rested beside the dying camp fire. Zelda was a lump buried under the buffalo robe, snoring softly. I stoked the night fire and boiled a noggin of bark tea, then slept huddled in the greatcoat, propped just inside the front corner of the shelter, one eye on the horses, the other watching the river approach to camp whenever I wakened and checked fire and horses.

In the coldest part of night before false dawn I fed, watered, and saddled the horses. The chill wind dipped and swirled, and a solid gray overcast of clouds domed the sky. The weather would break today before nightfall if not sooner.

I poked Zelda awake with my rifle barrel. "Overslept again, didn't you? Won't never learn, will you now?" I teased, pulling at the bottom of the buffalo robe and uncovering her head.

She sat upright and rubbed sleep from her eyes with both hands. "Don't be mean. Ain't fair throwin' a body's own words at her this early."

I passed her the noggin and a pan of fried meat. "We leave shortly. Eat quick and see to yourself round back. I'll load the horses."

We handled calls of nature like a man and woman who'd been together years rather than days. Hard things always seemed easy for us but the smallest thing pushed us apart, a problem I'd thought about since our first meeting. I was beginning to suspect I contributed as much to our personal squabbles and misunderstandings as she did, not that I'd ever admit being at fault to anyone changeable as Zelda.

She returned, robe-coat dwarfing her slim body, and watched me load the furs on the last horse in line. Once she was astride the lead horse, I tied her feet and pointed at the sky. "Rain or snow before we reach Wallace Ridge and the cave." From a greatcoat pocket I pulled a wide swatch of soft buckskin I'd cut from the bottom of my hunting frock. "Tie this on your head when you need it. It'll shed water better'n a flat rock." She stuffed the leather scarf in the front of her coat.

Next I handed across the pistol I'd recovered from her bed. "It's primed and ready. Keep it dry." The weapon disappeared inside the robe-coat too.

I stepped against the shoulder of her horse. "Sooner or later the Ballard party will be following along behind us. They might even make a dash for the fort to beat the weather home, so we've got to outrun

them. We're traveling far as yesterday, only faster
since the trail's better." I laid hold of her sleeve and
said, "Whatever happens, don't ask questions. Watch
me and do only what I tell you. No matter how bad
it gets, even if we abandon the horses, the larder, the
furs, all of it, we keep going straight for your paw's
cabin. You understand?"

She nodded twice and settled in the packsaddle.
"I'm with you all the way round the bend, tall man,
never fear." With a sly grin, she knuckled her
forehead.

Satisfied I had her attention, I heaped snow on the
embers in the fire pit with a bark slab; they hissed
and a wave of steam rose. I shoveled snow till the
embers were completely buried, killing any chance
the wind would rekindle them. That was all that
could be done to forestall quick discovery and pursuit. There was no hiding the signs of our overnight
stay or the shod tracks and droppings of the horses.
Once on our trail, we'd be no harder to follow than
your nose. I prayed for snow instead of rain.

Full dawn brought yellowish light far eastward at
the bottom edge of the gray cloud cover. The heavy
clouds masked the sunrise, and the morning turned
gloomy and dank. Steady as the march of time, the
chill wind blew without letup, backing around from
west to due south. Mean weather was in the offing
and we were headed into it.

I guided the pack train southward along the
western side of the high ground flanking the Muskingum, staying off the skyline. Toward midday, well

away from the Ballard camp, far enough even the
noise of our passage was beyond earshot, I angled
upward onto the Injun pathway atop the high ridge
line overlooking the Muskingum to take advantage
of that worn trail.

A few drops splattered my hat brim and sleet
commenced. I stopped the horses and looked back at
Zelda. She was tying the buckskin scarf over her
muslin headband. I fished jerked meat, the last of
Abel's pemmican, and a jug from the larder horse for
the nooning.

We ate where we were, she astride, me flat-footed
beside her horse. A couple of slugs of Monongahela
whiskey fanned a teary sparkle in Zelda's eyes and
burned my throat. The sleet slackened, then quit.
But it was only a short respite, not the end of
anything. The sky darkened as we watched.

I lashed the whiskey jug to Zelda's saddle. "Case
you need it," I explained. "Like before, lessen you
give out with a whoa, we don't stop for even the
devil's due till we reach the cave. Ain't any norther
movin' in, but it'll be nasty and cold nevertheless."

And with that, I clucked the lead horse ahead and
set off at a near trot.

The storm held its breath a short while. Then
darker clouds forged from the southwest and the
sleet began anew, icy pellets so wet and heavy they
grabbed hold of cloth and horsehair without bouncing off. A layer of frozen slush soon coated our heads
and shoulders and the pack animals with their high
saddles. The trail became slick and slowed our pace.

Daylight dwindled even though sunset and dusk were a ways off yet.

The earlier gray overcast was completely gone, replaced by roiling clouds of deepest black bringing with them ever stronger winds that tugged hard at my hat brim. Off southwest a deep rumble sounded on high, then rolled toward us. Zelda yelped in surprise. A jagged bolt of lightning zapped downward, followed by another ponderous rumble. Zelda yelped a mite louder.

The trail dipped and turned and wound around a rock shoulder that sealed off the wind. I halted the pack train for a blow and moved back beside Zelda. She clawed sleet from her buckskin scarf and raised the jug for a slug of Monongahela. "Scary, right scary," she observed.

"Thunder-snow," I told her.

She raised eyebrows crusted with ice.

"Never seen it myself, but Uncle Jeremiah talked about it. Just like a summer thunderstorm, only it don't rain. It snows, snows a heap, then turns powerfully cold. Hunters have been soaked clean through to the skin, then frozen stiff as boards."

Zelda wiped a red and runny nose. "So will we, lessen we hole up in your cave. How much farther?"

I told her straight, no holds barred. "Till after full dark at least. We've no druthers. We'll skirt a ravine ahead where I camped comin' upriver but the horses can't make it down in there."

Zelda braced herself and took a last swallow of

corn liquor. She hung the jug back on her saddle and motioned for me to tie her hands fast. "I'm dog-tired. Go quick as you can. I'm cold clean to the bone already."

We taken out again.

Lightning flashed repeatedly, thunder crashed and rolled. The slashing bursts of white light and ear-splitting rumbles upset the horses. They snorted and trembled, and it took all my strength and guile to keep them lined out and under control. They shook sleet from their heads and plodded onward. I admired their heart and bottom and thanked the Lord I had them; I was too worn down for carrying Zelda, who couldn't walk a rod on her own.

Even after we'd skirted the ravine and traveled in full darkness, lightning and thunder continued and wet snow replaced the sleet. The wind backed off a notch but grew colder. My feet were numb inside frozen moccasins by the time we neared the Wallace Ridge cave.

Zelda's head was hidden by the collar of the buffalo robe coat and she sagged low in the saddle, still astride only because I'd tied her fast.

I never did tell her I led the horses plumb past our destination. A streak of lightning revealing white blazes on the dark trunks bordering the trail saved our bacon.

The trail being too narrow for swinging the pack train about, I tied the lead horse to a tree, untied Zelda and carried her back past the train. She had enough strength left to wrap her arms round my neck.

The cave entryway was a dark hole amidst a jumble of gray rock. No firelight shown from within and I couldn't smell smoke. It was deserted but a real surprise awaited, a real godsend. Someone, likely the Ballard party, had replaced the wood I'd burned and cleaned the water bowl.

I laid Zelda on the pounded dirt floor, unslung Abel's rifle from my back, and started a fire the surest way I knew, plugging the touchhole and igniting a wad of tow in the pan with spark and powder. Flames were leaping and snapping before Zelda moaned and opened her eyes.

I pulled her upright, gently slapped icy cheeks, and helped her out of the robe-coat. Her frock was dry. The bottoms of her breeches that hung below the coat were frozen hard as rock. I swung her feet nearer the fire and removed her tall leather moccasins. "Rub your feet till they're good and warm. I'll be back with vittles and bedding."

I unstrung the pack animals and hobbled them in place. They began lipping the wet snow, ignoring the last of the lightning and thunder. I dropped their loads beside them, but left them saddled with eased cinches. They'd huddle together and ride out the snowstorm; they were a toughened lot. Shouldering the larder bundles, I edged round behind them.

Lightning flashed and in that brilliant moment, through the easing curtain of snow, I saw far back up the trail past the cave and a familiar shape stopped me dead in my tracks, for there in the middle of the worn pathway, rifle held across his chest, pelt cap glittering with ice, sparse beard matted into a black lump hanging from his long white face, stood Timothy Ballard.

Chapter 18

As sure as I'd seen him, he'd seen me.

I shielded my body with the larder bundles and lumbered for the cave. I shoved the bundles inside and grabbed Abel's rifle. Zelda's head snapped around. "Company. Don't know how many, only saw one. If I don't call out, shoot the next body through the door hole." And with that brief warning I had the rifle primed and was gone again.

I scampered behind a thick trunk twixt the cave and the horses. From there the northern trail shown clearly in the next lightning bolt.

Timothy Ballard was gone.

The oldest Ballard brother was wilier than smoke. He'd been tracking us and knew someone traveled with me. In the darkness following the lightning flashes he couldn't be certain where I'd gone or where my partner might be or what we might be planning in response to his sudden appearance. Timothy—and anyone backing him—had found cover and watched close as owls.

The lightning and thunder ended. I desperately

wanted to stamp some warmth into my feet but stayed dead quiet, listening close since the snow limited what could be seen without lightning to a few feet in the black dark of night. I snugged the beaded cover over the lock of Abel's rifle and hunkered down. They couldn't get behind me without my hearing them, and if they moved in front of the cave entryway, I'd spot them against the faint light of the fire showing from inside.

It was a standoff of the worst kind. We could all stick behind cover awaiting a telltale move on the other's part that might present a target or permit an attack with hand weapons. And if neither side moved a lick, we'd all freeze solid by morning.

I lost all feeling in my feet and shivers racked me. The weather forced me into the open. Maybe I'd be ambushed when I stepped from the cave in the morning, but I'd at least spend my last night warm, with a full belly before departing this ol' world. I sidled over to the cave entryway and softly called Zelda's name.

She didn't answer. When she didn't hear a second soft call, I plunged inside, too cold to wait any longer, breath held in anticipation of the coming shot.

I needn't have fretted. She'd wedged herself between the woodpile and the wall of the cave beyond the fire, the farthest point from the entryway, and gone fast asleep, pistol clamped between bent knees. A hard tug freed the pistol and I uncocked the weapon while she slept without awakening.

My greatcoat made a decent bed by the fire and I moved her gently there. I added wood to the burned-down flame and had a good look-see. Her forehead was hot and wet and her skin had that sickly pallor of the fever-ridden. Our circumstances had hit rock bottom.

I checked the load and priming of Abel's rifle and the pistol, laid hand weapons close by, then boiled venison for broth while I rubbed bare feet, facing the entryway all the while.

All was quiet outside except for occasional hoof stamping and a snort or two by the horses. They were miserable and hungry, beset by a wet, cold snow that wouldn't taper off or stop altogether for hours.

No challenge rent the dark night. No armed enemy appeared anywhere near the entryway. The standoff continued, but at least I'd warm feet and a belly full of hot meat and broth, both of which made clear thinking easier.

Timothy Ballard and whoever sided him had better sense than to attack through the narrow entryway where they'd be shot one at a time or tomahawked. Maybe I'd food and a spring for water in here, but sooner or later food ran out and, if all else failed, they'd starve us into submission without suffering any harm themselves.

That was tomorrow. Tonight was a different story. Unless they wanted to freeze to death, they'd withdraw beyond rifle range and build a fire and hold on through the night. At daylight they'd lay siege to the place and forever hold the upper hand.

The prospect of a siege come daylight left one possible way out: load the horses and make a dash for it in the middle of the night before the Ballards and their friends were in place with loaded rifles trained on the entryway. A running fight in the dark beat a one-sided siege every time.

Much argued against a bold, half-mad dash in the middle of the night. The horses were worn down and might prove balky. Darkness and wet snow made ridge line travel extremely dangerous. The biggest drawback was Zelda. She was hot and sweaty and likely feverish. The strain of such a nighttime trek through the wet and cold was more than she could withstand, might even kill her. The wounds inflicted by Abel's knife had scabbed over nicely but left a mighty weakened woman in their wake. If she went with me, it might be tantamount to shooting her.

Lord, nothing was ever simple and straightforward where this girl-woman was concerned. If I broke my promise and left her behind, she'd fall into the hands of the Ballards. If I stayed with her, I was a dead man once we reached Fort Frye for I'd no proof to offer my fellow settlers and stay the hangman's hand.

Zelda stirred and raised her head. "What happened? Where they be?"

"Likely crowded around a fire back the trail a ways, waiting for daylight."

Zelda was no fool. "We'll be trapped in here, won't we now? No way out for you."

She turned on her side and lay facing me. "What're we goin' to do, Matthan?"

"Sit here and stay warm, eat like wolves, and surrender come daylight. That's all there is to it, girl. I'll die with a full belly and they'll fetch you home to your paw. They're a mean lot but they'd not dare touch you. The colonel would have them horse-whipped for sure."

Her green eyes bored into me and she grew stern round the mouth. "I'll not have them near me, I told you that, didn't I? After all, you promised, didn't you?"

I set the noggin in front of her. "They'll not bother you with me a prisoner. The colonel'll want me alive for a big show when he hangs me, never you fear."

She ignored the hot broth. "What would you do if I wasn't here, Matthan? You wouldn't laze about and let them take you easy as all get out, would you now?"

No point in lying here, I thought. "No, I'd load the horses and taken down the trail like a crazed buffalo and charge right through them that got in my way. Might get shot but I'd have my chance thataway."

Her answer was snake-quick. "Then we'll run for it together."

My mouth dropped open. "You're too sick for such a ride. You couldn't see it through."

A blush colored her features and it wasn't from

fever or embarrassment. "Damn it, Matthan, I'm tired of menfolk always spoutin' off 'bout what I can or can't do. That's all my brothers and Paw ever done to me. But I did everything I wanted anyways and the hell with what they and other folks thought. You said it before: crazy as a loon. I know that's what they say 'bout me, but I don't flat give a damn." She halted and sucked in some wind. "Do you understand what I'm sayin', tall man?"

"Sounds like I'm leaving here in the middle of the night and you're riding with me. If you die somewhere down the trail, you're trusting me to give you a decent burial. That about it."

"That it be. But I'm expectin' I'll be delivered to my paw's very door, just like you promised. If you abandon me 'fore we get there, I'll never forgive you. I'll haunt you in hell, tall man. Trust me, I can do it."

And with that sworn statement she fell back on the greatcoat.

I sat speechless.

She spoke at the ceiling but I heard every word. "I'm fussy 'bout how I'm fetched home. When folks believe you unladylike and crazy-minded enough you talk with birds, a girl has only her pride to hang on to, don't you know."

I realized at that very moment I loved her more than life, would always love her, even if I never saw her again after tonight. She was all a woman could be or need be for a man. She was your own heart beating.

Before I could tell her that, she broke the silence. "Well, load your damn horses while I eat. Time be a-wastin'. I've slept long enough and won't feel any better if'n we wait till mornin', which we can't." She forced herself upright and reached for the noggin, impatient now she'd made her decision. "Git, tall man. I'll be ready when you be."

The cold without my greatcoat was shocking. Snow fell with a wet hiss. The horses were bunched tightly for warmth. I cracked ice from their heads with the handle of my knife and separated them enough for cinch tightening and loading. They smelled action and came alert, tired enough to be restless and unfriendly, but too well-trained for outright rebellion. Under a firm hand they lined out for travel.

I scouted the ridge line a short distance in both directions. If the Ballards were still around, they'd withdrawn a doubly safe distance for their night fire. We'd at least get under way without a fight. Unless their brains had dried up and blown away with the wind, they'd be waiting downtrail, the direction of our travel all day.

Zelda was bundled in the buffalo robe and tall moccasins with buckskin scarf covering her head. The larder bundles had been repacked with her kettle tied securely atop the pile. She stuffed the pistol in her coat and waited for me to speak.

"Same as before. Stay low and shoot late as you can. Be ready if I slap that horse's rump hard and send you on ahead. I'll catch you, just don't you stop for any reason." She bobbed her head, not bothering to knuckle her forehead as before. We were about a serious undertaking and she treated it as such.

I donned the greatcoat, belted knife, tomahawk, and shot pouch round my middle and said, "I'll load our larder. Throw every last piece of wood on the fire. We want it burning and smoking all night long."

In short order Zelda sat astride her horse. I made a last quick check of loads, straps, cinches, and any loose, clanking gear, then fisted the lead rein. "We'll move easy and quiet for a few miles and maybe get clear of them."

I led off and in hissing snow with enough wind to ripple my hat brim, we gave off little noise. The fire-lighted cave entryway slipped away behind us. It was as black as night as I ever remembered. I found the trail more by feel than sight.

I reckoned it a little past the midnight hour. We covered considerable ground before Zelda tugged at my coat shoulder. "Tie me aboard, Matthan. I'm slippin' down."

I was glad I couldn't see her in the darkness. Her wearied tone sparked a heap of guilt. She was offering everything she had to save my life, something one expected only of blood kin. When she cared, her feelings ran deep and true forever.

She thumped the horse's side with her foot and jerked me back to the business at hand. "Let's not tarry," she said quietly.

We wound across the Wallace Ridge trail unchallenged. Wherever the Ballards had their fire, in the darkness and heavy snow, neither of us saw or heard the other. Much later, beyond the roaring waters of Big Rock and strung out along the shortcut from Big Rock to Wolf Creek, I was elated over our good fortune. We'd somehow wriggled off the Ballards' hook and made a clean getaway. Leastways till they discovered the cave was empty.

A faint smudge showed on the eastern horizon, heralding a cold, wet, gray, downright miserable dawn. The snowfall began to taper off. Zelda's appearance in the first light of day was worse than at any time since Abel's attack. She burned with fever, her nose ran, and her breath rasped deep in her chest. She'd ridden all night without rest or ever stepping down. She was too tired to shake clinging snow from her scarf and coat. Her head lifted and she asked through clenched teeth, "How close be I to home, Matthan?"

"Not far, not far," I assured her.

"Don't stop," she mumbled. "I'll never get aboard again."

The horses needed prodding even though the snow halted altogether. The animals bearing the furs and larder had suffered the most. Zelda and the silver cache were less of a burden and those two horses plodded along with heads steady.

I halted when the ridge line petered out and the trail made a sharp descent to the bank of Wolf Creek. A mile or so downstream on the opposite bank sat the Shaw cabin. I untied Zelda's hands and feet. She tilted her head and looked with one eye. "Hang tight, girl. This horse is plumb tuckered, and if he falls, he'll roll on you for sure. I'm not losing you within shouting distance of your stoop."

She had enough presence of mind to lean down twixt the saddle trees and grab the horse's mane with both hands. She wagged her head and I coaxed the lead horse forward. The pack train followed in short, careful steps.

At the bottom of the ridge the trail dipped into a clearing and ran along the creek, then rose upward onto a bench of higher ground. Zelda's horse lunged up the incline and stumbled on loose stone at the edge of the bench, tugging backward on the reins. I spun to see if the untied Zelda was still astride, and a voice behind me with the ring of iron in it said, "Freeze right thar!"

I jerked the lead horse onto flat ground and turned about slowly, Abel's rifle held high, barrel pointing at the sky. Timothy Ballard blocked the trail, rifle stock lodged against his cheek, muzzle centered on my chest.

The packhorse stopped hard against my right arm. A second voice, on the left, said with unguarded glee, "Taken him just liken you planned we would, didn't we, Brother Timothy?"

I ignored Joseph Ballard and fixed my gaze on Timothy. The older brother was in charge here and Joseph would follow his orders.

We stared at each other. Timothy took a long chew on a mouthful of tobacco and said, "Been a fearsome night but well worth it, Matthan. The colonel'll be right happy to see ya."

He dipped his head to spit and I felt Zelda's foot thump the packhorse's ribs. The horse blew in surprise and stepped forward, bumping me aside.

"Watch out!" Joseph yelled in alarm.

Zelda rose in the saddle, her hand emerged from the front of her coat, I heard the double click of a cocking pistol, and the pistol fired a split-second before Timothy's rifle boomed. Zelda jerked and fell toward me. I ducked down to catch her and Joseph fired. The ball buzzed past my ear and struck the packhorse in the neck. My rifle hit the snow as I caught Zelda and reared clear of the reeling, bleeding horse.

A quick glance confirmed Timothy was down, hit hard. I laid Zelda on the ground. The wounded horse neighed in pain and veered twixt Joseph and me.

The animal collapsed on his knees and Joseph saw me across the horse's back, upright and unhurt. He panicked, threw his rifle down, and reached for a pistol stuck behind his belt, drawing backhanded. I swept up Abel's rifle and charged, howling like mad. Joseph did get the hammer drawn back as he drew, but before he could level the pistol and fire, I bashed him with my rifle barrel alongside his bandaged jawbone. His head snapped sideways, the pistol slipped from his hand, and he sagged against my chest. I pushed him away and he flopped into the snow, both hands clutching his rebroken face.

I was frantic with worry about Zelda but didn't rush to her. I cocked my rifle and approached Timothy carefully. He lay on his back. His chest pumped and I knew he was alive. I tossed his gun into the bushes and knelt beside him. A bloody furrow wide as my thumb ran clean down the side of his head. He'd be down and out a goodly while, then sick and dizzy for days.

I rushed to Zelda, who sprawled facedown. Blood spotted her coat sleeve above the elbow. I turned her over gently and cradled her slight body in my arms. Her eyes slowly opened. "Did I hit him?"

"Yeah, you hit him. He's not dead, but he won't fight any more this day. Joseph's not fit for anything more either."

The packhorse flattened and a final breath rattled in his throat. "My arm hurts," Zelda said.

I slid her coat open. The ball had passed through the fleshy part of the upper arm, missing the bone. The bleeding had stopped already.

"It'll pain you some but not kill you," I told her, pulling her coat in place.

She coughed hard and deep. There was a rumbly sound in her chest that scared me.

I rose, set her on wobbly legs, and knelt in front of her. Favoring her wounded arm, she settled on my back and wound her good arm round my neck. "Just like old times, eh, tall man?"

She hung tight while I cut the rope tying the dead

horse to the rest of the pack train and plucked Abel's rifle from the snow.

"Take me home, please," Zelda whispered in my ear, and we headed downstream.

I left the Ballard brothers where they lay.

Chapter 19

The ford short of the Shaw cabin flowed knee-deep.
I guided the pack train across its gravelly bottom.
Ice-cold water filled my moccasins and soaked the
legs of my breeches, nearly taking my breath away.
I slipped on the frozen bank and jerked Zelda. She
moaned and tightened her hold on me. The rearmost
packhorse scrambled out of the water and we approached her home at last.

"Yell for Paw so the dogs don't attack you," Zelda
cautioned.

The Shaw hounds began barking and growling as
they spotted us. I halted the horses. Smoke billowed
from the cabin chimney. Her paw was to home.

"Call off the dogs or I'll shoot your daughter," I
yelled.

In no time atall a rifle barrel slid between door
and jamb. A bearded face could be seen in the narrow
opening.

"Who be there?"

"Matthan Hannar," I answered. "I've brought your

daughter home. She's hurt and poorly. Call off those dogs," I commanded.

Zebulon Shaw stepped through the doorway onto the stone stoop.

Zelda squirmed about and got her head above my shoulder. "Call 'em off, Paw. I be home at last," she called and fainted dead away.

Zeb cursed and flailed with his rifle barrel and drove the hounds into submission at the side of the cabin. He leaned his gun against the doorjamb and came toward me in a lurching run.

We said nothing more. He lifted Zelda from my back, then carried her into the cabin without a backward glance. I watched the door swing shut.

The lead horse tossed his head and I led the three remaining pack animals round the cabin opposite the growling, panting hounds to Zebulon's horse shed. A fine chestnut gelding thrust a blazed face over a gated enclosure next to the open-sided shed and whinnied a welcome. I'd heard tales of Zelda's personal mount but never before laid eyes on him. Little wonder she rode astride; he was too powerful to handle from a sidesaddle.

I unloaded the pack train, removed their saddles, and watered them at the stone trough. They tanked up and drifted into the shed to feed on cut cane and meadow hay. I patted and chatted quietly with the gelding. He was well muscled and deep in the chest, clean-limbed everywhere. He'd run a far distance without tiring.

Suddenly, I was bone-tired everywhere, nigh onto

dropping flat in my own tracks. But sleep was a long ways off yet for Matthan Hannar.

I left the fur bales and larder piled before the shed and toted the two pouches of silver and Abel's rifle across the dooryard. I entered without knocking.

A fire blazed in the hearth. Stew, the most delicious smell under the sun, bubbled and steamed in a hanging kettle. Bread browned in a baking niche. I almost expected Mother to speak to me.

"You're supposedly dead or long gone down the Ohio," Zebulon said from a dim corner. He'd placed Zelda on a rope bed and covered her.

I laid the silver pouches on the squat table centering the room and moved before the fire, aching for warmth on my wet feet.

"How is she?"

"Asleep and her arm's not bleeding. She swallowed a little whiskey." He spun on his stool and faced me squarely.

"Who shot her?"

"Timothy Ballard."

A frown knitted his brow. "He cut her bad too?"

"No, Abel Stillwagon, just before I killed him. But that's a long story and she'll tell it sometime. I'm too damn tired for yarning."

Zebulon brought me the whiskey jug. "Shed them moccasins and take a chair. You look more tucked up than an overrode horse," he said, leaning to stir the contents of the hanging kettle.

He set a trencher heaped with stew and a thick wedge of fresh bread on the table. I ate in gulps, washing it all down with dollops of whiskey. Warmed the soul right smartly, his vittles did. I swiped my mouth clean with a coat sleeve and took a final slurp of Monongahela.

"Mr. Shaw, we need to palaver. But first let me show you something."

I opened and spread wide the mouth of a silver pouch and beckoned him from Zelda's dim corner. With one look his eyes widened and his mouth pursed. A man didn't have opportunity to often see anything that valuable in a whole lifetime. Then his face darkened and he started to speak, "If you—"

"Let me talk before you fly off the handle," I snapped.

It took a whale of an effort, but he bit his lip and fixed me with a ferocious glare. Zebulon wasn't used to an affront of any kind or orders from others in his own cabin. Only Zelda escaped his wrath when he had a fire in his stack.

"Somehow Stillwagon traded the Injuns for these silver pieces or he stole them. That doesn't matter. He had them with him when we rendezvoused, along with two bales of prime pelts. The pelts I piled by the horse shed. . . . Now, we had a set-to with the Ballard brothers not over an hour ago and Zelda shot Timothy and I broke Joseph's jaw again."

With that Zebulon plunked down in a chair opposite me and hung on my every word.

"Sooner or later, those brothers will stumble over to Fort Frye and rouse the whole countryside or follow us here, hell-bent on revenge. Either way you

might have to buy them off and shut them up about
Zelda siding with me. The pelt bundles should
button their lips. You talk real well, Mr. Shaw. You
can refuse ill-gotten gains and let them brothers
bustle off happy as foxes in a henhouse. You follow
me?"

Zebulon nodded and helped himself to a long pull
on the jug while I went on speechifying.

"I'm not long for this part of the country. I'm not
about to stretch a rope for something I didn't do, and
I've no means of proving my innocence. Jeremiah,
Step-paw, and Abel are all dead. So who's to believe
Matthan Hannar's story?"

"No one, most likely," Zebulon agreed.

"All right, here's my proposition. You keep that
pouch for you and your daughter. In return, you give
me that chestnut gelding. I need to make some fast
tracks before dawn tomorrow. After that, they'll
never lay hold of me."

Zebulon stared silently for a good long while.
From the dim corner Zelda called his name from her
sickbed.

He went over there, sat on his stool, and a heated
exchange of words took place. Finally, he cast a long
sigh and returned to the table.

"My daughter says you're to have the chestnut.
She's accepting your proposition. She claims she'd
not be alive if you hadn't fought those Injuns and
killed Abel and his partner and brung her home,
Ballards or no Ballards."

Zebulon had a sick cast on his face.

"And Zed and Zeb?" I asked.

He nodded sadly. "She told me 'bout them too."

"Mr. Shaw, they died fighting. They'll never know they helped save Zelda as much as I did. I couldn't whip that many Injuns alone. They drew them off and gave me my chance. They were true brothers to the end."

"That's better'n nothing, I guess," Zebulon admitted begrudgingly.

I slipped into damp but warm moccasins and checked rifle and hand weapons. Zelda's father remained at the table with the whisky jug, shocked by the stunning news he had his precious daughter home once more, but at the cost of his two sons, a mean bargain at best.

I crossed to the rope bed. Zelda was buried beneath a heavy quilt. She extended a slim bare arm and I grasped her fingers. "It was a hell of a venture, girl, one I'll never forget. I owe you my life."

Green eyes homed in on me. "I only follow my heart, Matthan. . . . Maybe sometimes it's too big for me and everyone else."

"Not hardly, not hardly," I stammered. I leaned over and kissed her forehead.

"Good-bye, Zelda, my love," I squeezed past the lump in my throat.

"See, Matthan," she said softly, "just like I been tellin' you, it not be a hard name atall."

I straightened with a long, last look at her bronze features, fine mouth, and man-taming eyes, turned, nodded a silent good-bye to Zebulon, and walked from the cabin with the unopened silver pouch and Abel's rifle, never looking back.

They were the hardest steps I ever took. But I shed no tears. I'd learned crying didn't help. The pain and loss still burned inside a man when he finished. Only the Lord and the passage of time did any real healing.

The snowy pathway we'd covered on our arrival was deserted. Timothy and Joseph had forsworn more fighting for the moment. They'd headed for Fort Frye, and given their wounds and hurts, they'd be a while getting there.

No barking or growling came from the creek side of the cabin. Fear of another beating held the Shaw hounds at bay.

I bridled and saddled the gelding, tied the silver pouch behind the seat, led him clear of the gated enclosure, and mounted. From the gelding's back I spied Zelda's infernal cooking pot atop the bundled larder I'd unloaded earlier. I kneed the gelding close and snatched up the kettle.

I lingered, rubbing the smooth metal, and remembering. But the chestnut had no interest in past events and pranced sideways, impatient to run. I reined him over in front of the cabin, reached down and placed Zelda's precious pot on the stone stoop where Zebulon couldn't help but find it.

Then I rode westward for the Ohio.

Epilogue

Marietta, Ohio
February 26, 1836

My dearest son,
Matthan Hannar, Jr.,

The pages bearing your name in my safe at the boatyard tell the story of what truly happened in the winter of 17 and 92 as best an old man in his final days can remember it.

Perhaps if I last the final weeks of this damnably cold winter besetting us, I might write down for you all that happened after I rode out of the Shaw yard some forty odd years ago.

Perhaps I should tell how I traded part of the Injun silver and the gelding for a flatboat over in Indiana territory, lured aboard a motley crew I captained at rifle point, and slipped on south down the Ohio and Mississippi to that great port of dreams— New Orleans.

You might enjoy reading about the thundering lightning storm that sank the flatboat and fetched me ashore on the banks of the De Montaine plantation, soaked to the gills and clutching my precious pouch of silver, a wild night that changed my life and what came to be yours forever, for the brave soul who rescued me was none other than Monsieur De Montaine himself.

My, what a wise and generous benefactor the Monsieur came to be. He first took me into his home

and made me a shipbuilder, then a company partner.
He saw to the schooling I desperately needed and
later introduced me to a dark and lustrous beauty,
Ravanna, whom I eventually married and with
whom I sired you, may she forever rest in peace.

I must set forth too my chance encounter with the
great border fighter Tice Wentsell on the battlefield
at New Orleans during the tussle of 18 and 15 when
I lost a foot to wound and rot.

You should know it was Tice Wentsell who wrote it
all down, how he found the remains of Stillwagon
and Hasper in the ashes of the rendezvous tree and
trailed us south, arriving at the Shaw cabin two
days after I rode off, there to get the rest of the
particulars from Zebulon Shaw as Zelda had told
them. And once the redoubtable Wentsell finished
his report, he delivered it to General Putnam at
Marietta and cleared my name, at least in the eyes
of the law.

I'll go to my grave owing Tice Wentsell. His report,
the statement of a ranger whose word went unchallenged the whole of the Ohio backcountry, declared
me blameless of trading with the Injuns and sundry
other crimes. Without such a public declaration of
my innocence, I'd never have dared return with you
and your mother in 18 and 19 and build the Marietta
yards of HANNAR AND DE MONTAINE, SHIPBUILDERS AND
FREIGHT AGENTS, EXTRAORDINAIRE. Tidy profits, after all,
seldom shorten the long arm of the gendarmes.

My recounting must end here for the winter. My

hand grows feeble, the quill heavy as lead. My strength fades long before the light of each day.

I have, howsomever, one final heart-wrenching favor to ask of you, never minding if that favor might ruin your deepest feelings for me.

At Cheyney's Crossing over the Ohio in Virginia, a respected and fair-haired lady of considerable years owns a wayside inn and tavern named The Tall Man. The owner was never betrothed but turned up at the Crossing in 17 and 93 with an infant child.

This dear woman is never to know want, I beg of you.

Pray, let me explain when explanation is most difficult. I learned many things from Tice Wentsell after our New Orleans reunion. He told me Zelda Shaw overcame her afflictions and birthed a child in the autumn of 17 and 92. Never turning cheek she purchased the inn at the Crossing and, alone, raised a fine son, a son she named Matthan Shaw, the same Matthan Shaw who superintends our Marietta yard, the same Matthan Shaw I'm at last admitting is, in truth, your half brother.

I hope and pray you will watch over Matthan Shaw and his family, and if necessary, his mother. Lord knows we can afford to offer sustenance for all those, few as they are, we hold near and dear.

Care for them, I ask of you. But tell Matthan Shaw nothing of his true beginnings. I trust you not to cower or embarrass him, but love him as a brother rather than from afar as I have, for I dare not claim him without violating his mother Zelda's wishes, which I will never do.

May the Lord guide you and help you through the surprises and deathbed revelations of an old he-goat such as me, who must pay for his past deeds, both fair and foul, so he can at least sleep a few nights without bad dreams.

No matter what you decide, I will love you no less, ever.

I only pray you can say the same for me, both now . . . and when I'm gone.

Godspeed, my favorite son.

As the Civil War raged in the South, the urgent call for doctors resounded in every corner of the nation. One family had the courage to answer the call.

THE HEALER'S ROAD
J.L. REASONER
• author of <u>Rivers of Gold</u> •

When his parents died because of a lack of proper medicine, Thomas Black vowed to become a doctor and better people's lives. Now, with the advent of war, he is challenged to provide better care than ever before—in a fraction of the time. During the savage conflict of the Civil War, Thomas Black, and his two children who follow in his footsteps, will embody the true nobility of the American spirit.

A Jove novel coming in October